Knightshade

also by Paul Féval
translated, annotated and introduced by
Brian Stableford

The Vampire Countess

Vampire City

Knightshade

(*Le Chevalier Ténèbre*)

by
Paul Féval

translated, annotated and introduced by
Brian Stableford

A Black Coat Press Book

Acknowledgements: I am indebted to Xavier Legrand-Ferronnière, who located a copy of the Marabout edition of *Le Chevalier Ténèbre* for me, and to Robert Morgan, whose Sarob Press provided the translation with its first home. I should also like to thank Jane Stableford and David McDonnell for proofreading the typescript.

Visit our website at www.blackcoatpress.com

Table of Contents

Introduction

Le Chevalier Ténèbre was the second of three novels by
Paul Féval which touch on the subject of vampirism,
although the notion is a less prominent feature therein
than it had been in *La Vampire* (1856; tr. as *The Vampire
Countess*) or was again to be in *La Ville-Vampire* (tr. as
Vampire City), which was written in 1867 although it did
not appear in book form until 1875. *Le Chevalier Ténèbre* also appeared in book form for the first time in
1875, but it had been serialized in *Le Musée des Familles* in 1860.

Féval was at the height of his fame in 1860, having
scored his greatest success three years earlier with *Le
Bossu* (*The Hunchback*), which seemed to its readers to
be pioneering a new kind of fiction that eventually came
to be called the "*roman de cape et d'épée*" (*novel of
cloak and sword*). *Le Bossu* was not a particularly original novel in terms of its content, much of which echoed
the work Féval had already done in his capacity as a pro-
lific *feuilletonist*–i.e. a writer of popular serial fiction–
before his career was interrupted in 1854 by health prob-
lems, and had been second-hand even then, borrowed
from more successful writers he was regularly commissioned to imitate, Alexandre Dumas and Eugène Sue.
What was new, however, was the tone of the story,
which clearly reflects the new spirit with which Féval
had been inspired following his recovery from illness

and his marriage to his doctor's daughter, Françoise Penoyée.

In 1846, Féval had published *Le Fils du Diable* (lit. *The Son of the Devil*, tr. as *The Three Red Knights*) which is, in essence, a combination of elements lifted from the plots of Dumas' most famous novels *Les Trois Mousquetaires* (1842-43; tr. as *The Three Musketeers*) and *Le Comte de Monte-Cristo* (1844-46; tr. as *The Count of Monte Cristo*), lightly seasoned with some borrowings from Sue's *Les Mystères de Paris* (1842-43; *The Mysteries of Paris*), the first great classic of the *roman feuilleton*. Like *Le Comte de Monte-Cristo*, *Le Fils du Diable* is a revenge fantasy in which retribution is carefully and cleverly, if somewhat belatedly, exacted upon the perpetrators of a dastardly crime, who have grown rich and powerful by means of its commission.

Whereas Dumas' hero is seeking revenge on his own behalf, however, Féval's three heroes are operating on behalf of a helpless child, who is the true heir to the legacy usurped by the master-criminal and his henchmen. Like *Les Trois Mousquetaires*, they operate on a principle of "all for one and one for all"–easily enough, given that they are brothers–but they have to do so in a more secretive manner, because they are supposed to be in jail. Throughout the story, they are working to a deadline because they have to get back into jail before anyone except their immediate custodian realizes that they are gone. They must, therefore, work in disguise, wearing masks over their faces whenever they are in danger of being recognized; to sow further confusion, they routinely dress in identical crimson costumes, so that no one will realize that they are three rather than one–thus giving what appears to others to be a single flamboyantly-dressed character a seemingly uncanny ability to be in two or three places at once. Sue's influence is seen in a romantic subplot involving the oldest brother with a humble but virtuous Parisian *demoiselle*, whose courtship is plagued by inconvenient obstacles and freakish misunderstandings.

When he set out to write *Le Bossu*, Féval obviously had it in mind to repeat this formula, but to do a much more thorough job. Again his hero, Lagardère, is faced with the task of protecting the true heir to a fortune that has been usurped by a murderous master-villain and his evil henchmen, and eventually ensuring that justice is done. There is only one of him this time, but he has authentically uncanny abilities; on the one hand, he has long made a living as an acrobat and actor, and on the other, he has the secret of a uniquely-effective fencing move, taught to him by the murdered father of his young ward (a girl, this time). Ironically, it is his *adoptée*'s knowledge of this move that reveals to the villain that he is still alive, launching a massive search; the only reason he has have lived long enough for the heroine to grow up is that his adversaries have previously taken it for granted that he perished in the climax of an earlier hunt. In order to recover the lost fortune, however, Lagardère is compelled to get close to the arch-villain, which he does by using his expertise as an actor to disguise himself as a hunchback, thus to exploit his adversary's superstitious attitude toward deformity. This echoes the key model to which Dumas and Sue had looked in formulating the conventions of the *roman feuilleton*, Victor Hugo, whose archetypal villain Claude Frollo was eventually brought down by Quasimodo in the 1828 classic *Notre-Dame de Paris* (tr. as *The Hunchback of Notre-Dame*).

Le Bossu is a much better book than *Le Fils du Diable* in several significant respects. Its fight scenes are far more extended and far more exciting. Its plot is much more complicated and suspenseful. Its portrait of Paris past–an essential element of great *romans feuilletons*–is more detailed and more atmospheric. Most important of all, though, is its breezy humor, which arises from its quasi-fabular quality.

The term "fabulation" has been reintroduced into modern critical theory by Robert Scholes, in *The Fabulators* (1967; revised as *Fabulation and Metafiction*, 1979), where he characterizes it as "ethically constrained fantasy" or "didactic romance" (other kinds of fantasy being "pure romance"). The key attribute of fabulation is a story's acute consciousness of its own artifice. The fabulator enters into a conspiracy with his reader which accepts that they both know perfectly well that they are participating in a fantasy–a construction intended to amuse, delight and educate–and that both of them are capable of appreciating the nature and quality of the artifice that goes into that process of construction. Unlike *Le Fils du Diable*, which presents itself straightforwardly as an account of events, *Le Bossu* involves the reader in its own artifice.

The other term Scholes uses in the final version of his book, metafiction, is defined as "experimental fabulation" and is used to refer to literary works whose ostentatious consciousness of their own fictitiousness involves the explicit redeployment of material from other texts, usually in order to identify and further explore their hidden subtexts. *Le Bossu* does this too, not merely reprocessing material from *Le Fils du Diable* that had borrowed from Dumas and Sue, who had borrowed some of it from Hugo, but taking it for granted that the reader will be conscious of that lineage and will take a connoisseur's pleasure in the manner and process of the redeployment.

By virtue of its fabular and metafictional qualities, *Le Bossu* is, in some ways, a very modern book–and its modernity reflects the fact that while Féval was participating with his fellow *feuilletonists* in the discovery and invention of the strategies and techniques of popular fiction, he was doing so in a self-conscious and intellectually interested manner. He was, in fact, quite fascinated by the mechanics, politics and psychology of storytelling, and by the teasing intricacies of the relationship between authors and audiences. *Le Bossu* displays these fascinations indirectly and implicitly, but they are the heart of its cavalier attitude to its own subject-matter. The temptation to make such issues manifest and address them more explicitly must, however, have been strong– and that is presumably why Féval elected to exploit his new marketability by writing a fabulation about fabulation, a metafiction of unprecedented convolution: *Le Chevalier Ténèbre*.

Knightshade displays some of Féval's weaknesses as conspicuously as it displays his main strengths, but it is undoubtedly one of the most interesting works in Féval's canon, and one whose substance is echoed in many half-hidden corners of the contemporary popular fiction marketplace. The novelist and critic Edmond Jaloux (1878-1949), one of Féval's many slightly-grudging admirers, opined that *Knightshade* would be a masterpiece of the fantastic if it were not written in "the drab and mock-pathetic language of the 19th century."

It seems highly probable that *Knightshade* was, like most serial novels of the period, made up as the writer went along, and by no means improbable that its author had no idea when he began it how long it would be allowed to run. (Popular *romans feuilletons* were extrapolated according to editorial command while those that failed to catch on were sometimes ruthlessly cut short.) It is, therefore, quite possible that the wayward course, peculiar structure and hurried finale of the narrative are largely matters of chance and circumstance–but, whether they were planned in advance or not, they have a definite propriety as well as a certain charm. The novella is, after all, explicitly written according to the "Galland formula."

Antoine Galland (1646-1715) was the Orientalist made famous by his early 18th-century translation of the Arabian Nights. That book established Scheherazade as the symbolic figurehead of all serial fiction, whose life would be forfeit if she were ever to let her husband retire to his bed without wanting to know what happened next. The tales she told him were always exaggerated, often fantastic and sometimes absurd, but they drew upon and helped to define the repertoire of tricks which storytellers routinely deploy in the interests of keeping their readers hooked. *Knightshade* is not the first *roman feuilleton* to have been planned according to that formula, and Féval must have been conscious of the irony of the fact that it suffered exactly the same fate as its most obvious predecessor and model, Alexandre Dumas' *Les Mille et Un Fantômes* (1849; *A Thousand and One Phantoms*). Indeed, he must have been conscious of a double symmetry, in that his earlier novel *La Vampire* had similarly mirrored the progress of the series begun with Dumas' *Joseph Balsamo* (1846-48; tr. as *Memoirs of a Physician*).

Joseph Balsamo–heavily influenced in its conception by Edward Bulwer-Lytton's occult classic *Zanoni* (1842)–had been intended to begin a projected series of novels about a serially-reincarnated sorcerer. It starts in fabulous style on Mont Tonnerre (*Mount Thunder*) where Balsamo receives his commission as the ultimate adversary of France after confronting the members of a secret society (presumably the Bavarian Illuminati) costumed as sword-bearing phantoms; Balsamo reveals himself to the chiefs of the organization as their long-awaited messiah, the Great Copt. As the serial progressed, however, Dumas gradually de-emphasized its supernatural component, probably in response to editorial pressure. Although Balsamo's ability to see the future with the aid of a virginal medium is crucial to the plot, the confused conclusion disposes of this scheme and Balsamo's occult mentor in a distinctly hasty manner.

The novel's immediate sequel, *Le Collier de la Reine* (1849-50; tr. as *The Queen's Necklace*), features the infamous life-style fantasist Count Cagliostro (whose real name was indeed Giuseppe Balsamo), but Cagliostro explicitly denies that he is Balsamo, and his similar powers of prophecy are conspicuously underused as the story unfolds; the plot and the denouement are almost entirely rationalized. *The Vampire Countess*, presumably laboring under similar editorial pressure, had likewise suffered a progressive de-emphasizing of its supernatural component *en route* to its final defiant hallucinatory flourish.

Just as Dumas had tried to find a more acceptable framework for supernatural fiction by employing the Galland formula and making the stories exemplary fictions told by and to urbane modern Parisians, so *Knight-*

shade sets out to represent its horror stories as stories told for the sake of thrilling a sophisticated audience–but Féval already knew that *Les Mille et Un Fantômes* had been strangled in its cradle after a bare handful of nights; most of the completed text was reissued in two volumes as *Une Journée à Fontenay-aux-Roses* (1849; lit. *A Day in Fontenay*, tr. as *Horror at Fontenoy*, Sphere, 1965) and *La Femme au Colliers de Velours* (1849; lit. *The Woman with the Velvet Necklace*, tr. as *The Pale Lady* or *The White Lady*), which contains the eponymous, oft-reprinted vampire story. It is, therefore, quite possible that *Knightshade* was actually planned to seem as if it had been interrupted and hurriedly aborted, by way of peculiar homage to Dumas. Whether that is true or not, it certainly set out from the very beginning to add one complication that Dumas had not: the storytellers who play Scheherazade in Féval's narrative, tell stories whose characters not only tell stories themselves, but continually resurface in their own stories as archetypal villains, masters of deception and disguise. This is no mere metafiction, but metametafiction, which leads the reader into an inescapable maze of infinite regress. The nested sequence of pretenses quickly becomes absurd, but its very absurdity is a commentary on the nature and seductive appeal of popular fiction. Perhaps it is "written in the drab and mock-pathetic language of the 19th century," but it is, in its own defiantly peculiar way, a masterpiece of the fantastic.

The author of *Knightshade* did not hesitate to accommodate the Galland formula to what was fast becoming the "Féval formula." That accommodation involved dissolving a tale apparently concerned with phantoms, brigands and vampires into a tale of bold but mundane criminal enterprise. Such a diminution is bathetic, and Féval is entirely conscious of that bathetic quality, but it is also what history had already accomplished–and the story makes much of that consciousness too.

The tale of the brothers Ténèbre's exploits as undead monsters, petty criminals and ingenious storytellers is so steadfast in its refusal to decide whether its supernatural apparatus is to be taken literally, metaphorically, or merely as a joke, that the drunken progress and hasty conclusion of the novella leave a great many pertinent questions unanswered–but that kind of playfulness is not at all inappropriate to the type of narrative it is, or to the time in which it was written. It is a story which continually raises questions about the terms on which storytellers may legitimately approach their audiences, and the way in which they manipulate those audiences, all the while exemplifying its own conclusions in its own approaches and manipulations. The narrative is full of nudges and winks, which seek–with a blithe disingenuousness that is actually rather ingenious–to establish that the reader is an active conspirator in the spinning of the story as well as a hapless victim of the spin.

The pioneering writers of popular serial fiction could hardly help being intensely interested in the question of what audiences required of their storytellers, and in the craftsmanship of keeping them hooked. Nor was that interest merely technical. There is a fascinating passage in Eugène Sue's *Les Mystères de Paris* set in La Force–the main prison of mid-19th century Paris–in which a petty thief must play Scheherazade, spinning out a story to hold an audience together in order to frustrate a scheme to murder an unjustly-imprisoned man. This storyteller points out–presumably echoing his own author's fascination with an equivalent discovery–that even thieves and outlaws love stories in which virtue triumphs and villainy is punished. His fellow prisoners–understandably–have no time at all for stories in which criminals much like themselves are seized by the police and sent to jail, but they retain a more profound sense of morality which gladly rejoices in the unusual punishment of the unusually wicked. Féval must have read this, and taken heed of the lesson it contained regarding the essential moral order of fiction–and he never tired of playing his own games with that moral order. *Knightshade* is one of the most intricate games of that sort ever produced, and was quite without precedent in 1860–but it is played, first and foremost, for fun.

Knightshade is a comedy, and is therefore entitled to require its readers not to take it too seriously, but beneath its comic surface lies a wondrously-convoluted tale of tale-making and tale-breaking which look back wryly at the mostly-accidental confusions of *Joseph Balsamo* and *The Vampire Countess*, and reproduce them deliberately, with a few extra twists thrown in for good measure. The manner in which the story continually calls its own narrative devices into question makes their evaluation–in both technical and moral terms–magnificently problematic. The initial presentation is calculatedly naive; the plot does not hesitate to employ clichés–but the accompanying commentary continually calls attention to the fact that they are clichés and the ironic narrative voice is always prepared to digress, if only momentarily, in order to discuss the circumstances of their effectiveness, or casually to insert a throwaway line about the possible symbolism of the motifs in question.

Knightshade was first published in the same year that Françoise Féval gave birth to Paul Féval *fils*, the son who was eventually to follow in his father's footsteps in more ways than one. The younger Paul not only became a popular writer but a writer whose career was built on metafiction. He wrote numerous sequels to his father's works–chronicling several further adventures of Lagardère–and also brought Dumas's most famous hero d'Artagnan together with Edmond Rostand's Cyrano de Bergerac (both characters had been based on actual persons) so that they could operate as a team. How proud the elder Paul would have been, as he wrote *Knightshade*, had he known that his as-yet-unborn son would carry forward its mission!

The younger Paul never became respectable, being regarded throughout his career as a mere hack inferior to his father, but the elder would not have held that against him; he never succeeded in being elected to the Academy himself, and had probably given up that hope by 1860, settling instead for inheriting the crown of feuilletonist-in-chief. (Sue had died in 1857, and Dumas's own quest for respectability had involved him more and more in the theatre). Féval was not the only claimant to that crown, however; his chief rival as a workaholic feuilletonist was now Pierre-Alexis Ponson du Terrail, thirteen years his junior. Although Ponson also wrote *La Baronne Trépassée* (1853; *The Late Baroness*), whose bizarre central character, teasing ambiguity and dreamlike accounts of vampiric activity undoubtedly influenced Féval's vampire novels, his main claim to fame was his creation of the flamboyant Rocambole, the hero of a long series of extravagant picaresque adventures–whose name was swiftly adapted into the adjective *rocambolesque* (meaning "far-fetched")–which he poured out in profusion from 1857 until his premature death in 1871.

Ponson's success emphasized one of the key discoveries made by the *feuilletonists* regarding the commodification of fiction. Sue had been the first to realize that the key to spinning out serials to vast length was the maintenance of a sense of threat, requiring vast webs of villainous intrigue in whose toils large numbers of innocent and unwitting victims could be trapped and tormented. The priority of such fiction was always on the villains and their conspiracies–a priority that Féval had reproduced and extended in such tales as *The Vampire Countess*. What Ponson illustrated very clearly, however, was that the interminable extension of a single serial like *Les Mystères de Paris* or *Le Juif Errant* (*The Wandering Jew*, Sue's other great success, serialized in 1844-5) was a strategy far inferior to the proliferation of a series of novels featuring the same central character. If the central character were to return again and again, though, he had to be the hero rather than the villain–at the very least, he had to be an outlaw whose victories could be celebrated, so that his return would always be welcome.

Lagardère was ultimately to become such a hero, courtesy of Paul Féval *fils*, but the elder Féval missed that opportunity, as he had earlier missed another in failing to exploit the character of Jean-Pierre Sévérin more fully in the two novels in which he had appeared– *La Chambre des Amours* (*The Chamber of Love*) and *The Vampire Countess*. He did, however, see the logic of the situation slightly more clearly than Ponson, realizing that if the crime-fighter had to replace the criminal at center-stage, and pull his weight in moving the plot along, then he would have to be more than an expert swordsman; he would also need to function as a would also need to function as a detective. Jean-Pierre Sévérin makes a tentative move in that direction when he sets off with a borrowed company of police agents to find his missing nephew in *The Vampire Countess*, but is not convincing in the role. It has to be admitted that Gaston de Lorgères in *Knightshade* is not that much better, in that his successes are largely founded on luck and he almost gets himself killed in consequence–he was not viable series material, and never reappeared–but he does qualify as another link in the chain that eventually generated the winning formula of popular fiction's central genre.

Although the phrase "*cape et d'épée*" eventually appeared in English, the first translation of *Le Bossu*'s most popular generic description was "cloak-and-dagger"–a term which can be applied to almost all of Féval's output after 1857, the year in which he produced the first of numerous crime stories set in the same historical period as *Knightshade*, *Les Compagnons du Silence* (*The Companions of Silence*), whose primary action takes place in 1823. His other principal production of 1860 was *Jean Diable*, a serial whose 1863 book version is now legendary for its rarity, but which made a crucial contribution to the development of crime fiction. It lent its title to a periodical, *Jean-Diable*, which became the first specialist magazine of crime fiction. It was while Féval was editing this magazine that he launched his own major series of crime novels, *Les Habits Noirs* (1863-75; *The Black Coats*), which eventually ran to seven novels in fourteen volumes. One of his editorial assistants, Émile Gaboriau, was subsequently to launch the rich tradition of the *romans policiers*, whose heroic detective, Monsieur Lecoq, reclaimed for the side of virtue the mastery of disguise possessed by the brothers

Ténèbre (and whose name is borrowed from another Lecoq, the chief henchman of the criminal mastermind of *Les Habits Noirs*).

Because it was a link in this chain, there is a sense in which *Knightshade* looks forward to the future–but recognizing that should not be allowed to blind us to the fact that it is also a deeply nostalgic book, regretful of the passing of the world in which it is set. It is, in some ways, a valedictory text. Féval's account of the metamorphoses of his villainous brothers refuses to pretend that their unmasking as petty criminals is anything but a drastic reduction of circumstances and charisma, but it does construe this reduction as part and parcel of a more general historical process; the underlying theme of the novella is the pattern of changes that had overtaken 19th century civilization between the time in which it is set and the time in which it was written. Not only does the narrative voice keep harking back to this matter, but, whenever it does so, its tone becomes much harsher– eventually descending as far as the remarkable hymn of hate that begins the final chapter. The way the story is set up is clearly intended to underline its study in historical contrasts. In order to understand this aspect of the story, the reader needs to be told certain things about its historical context.

The opening scene of *Knightshade* is drawn from actual history, and it is populated by a cast of characters who include two of the most important men of their era. The story is carefully and specifically dated, all its events taking place in the 1820s. Everything described therein–in Hungary as in Paris–had been obliterated by 1860, from which vantage-point the narrative voice is speaking. Féval chose to begin his story on the eve of the destruction of the social world featured in its chief setting by a corrosive process whose key event was the "July Revolution" of 1830.

The characters in the novella are, of course, unaware of what is soon to befall them, and their inability to respond to the obvious warnings contained in the tale of the brothers Ténèbre is a metaphorical reflection of their inability to see the real warning signs by which they must have been surrounded. The fundamental essence of the story is the tragically naive confidence of its exemplary characters in the aristocratic order reestablished by the Bourbon Restoration in the wake of Napoleon's second defeat.

Although we have long grown used to speaking of the French Revolution, meaning the one that took place in 1789, Paul Féval and his contemporaries did not think in those terms. The July Revolution of 1830 seemed highly significant to Féval not merely because he had actually lived through it, but because he believed that in casually overturning the ambitions of the Restoration it had put the final nail in the coffin of royal hegemony. In 1860, Féval was actually living under what is nowadays called the Second Empire, set up by Napoleon III in 1852; like the characters in his novella, he had no way of knowing that it was doomed to be obliterated ten years later by France's humiliating defeat in the Franco-Prussian War of 1870.

The Revolution of 1789 had been preceded by a remarkable upsurge of utopian philosophy and fiction, its potential most loudly advertised by Louis-Sébastien Mercier's *L'An 2440* (1771; *The Year 2440*), a pioneering vision of future Paris remade by the march of progress. By contrast, but with a certain revealing symmetry, the Revolution of 1830 was followed by a bitter reaction against the idea of progress, expressed in the sarcastic satirical fantasies of Charles Nodier–most notably *Hurlubleu, Grand Mantifafa d'Hurulubière* (1833) and its sequel *Leviathan le Long, Archikan des Paragons de l'Île Savante* (1833) and Émile Souvestre's pioneering anti-utopia *Le Monde tel qu'il sera* (1846; *The World As It Will Be*). Féval shared the disenchantment of these writers; the Parisian workers' revolt of 1848 and the election of Napoleon III might have delighted his fellow feuilletonist Eugène Sue, but they certainly did not delight him–and the coup in which the new Napoleon had established himself as Emperor had only served to increase his cynicism further.

In Féval's view, therefore, 1830 had been the year in which a new kind of darkness descended upon Europe; while enlightenment had banished the phantoms of old–including, in the observations of the novella's opening chapter, the dead who were reputed to rise from their graves along the banks of the Seine to haunt Paris– it had not contrived to deter a protean and proletarian class of irrepressible brigands, which operated on a world stage and would not rest until all the world's aristocratic treasuries had been looted and all the world's aristocratic bloodlines drained to extinction. This is the political subtext of *Knightshade*, which remains raw and sore in spite of all the novella's garish good humor and casual absurdity.

Conflans-l'Archevêque–i.e., the Archbishopric of Conflans–was still a village three miles south of Paris at the time when Féval was writing (it has, of course, long since been swallowed up by the city and is now a mere suburb). The place was, and still is, famous as the site at which Louis XI had signed the Treaty of Conflans in 1465, making crucial concessions to the so-called

22

"League of the Public Good," an alliance composed of the dukes of Bourbon, Brittany and Burgundy; the *château* at which the novella's two *soirées* take place was, however, destroyed only a few years after the time of the story.

The owner of the *château* featured in the story, Hyacinthe-Louis, Comte de Quélen (1778-1839) had become Archbishop of Paris in 1821 and had, as the text observes, achieved Féval's chief ambition of being elected to the Academy in 1824. He was indeed famed for his charity, and the picture of him painted by Féval seems reasonably accurate–but the narrator's sly observation that the Château of Conflans offered an open and level playing field to all shades of Royalist opinion has a deadly accuracy. The Archbishop's steadfast hostility to liberal reforms resulted in his archbishopric being sacked and looted in 1831–not, as the story casually alleges, "the day after the Revolution of July 1830" but certainly as a direct result of it. Ironically, that was also the year in which Archbishop de Quélen's reputation for charity reached its peak by virtue of his kindness to the poor during the cholera epidemic which arrived in Paris soon after the Revolution.

The second prelate featured in the story–the man who requests the Baron to tell his story–was almost as famous in his day as the Comte de Quélen. Denis, Comte de Frayssinous (1765-1841) became the official *aumônier du roi* in 1821 and was appointed Bishop of Hermopolis in 1822. He served as Minister of Ecclesiastical Affairs and Public Instruction from 1824 to 1828 but he retired to Rome in 1830, another victim of the July Revolution.

The other well-known victim of the Revolution numbered among the Archbishop's guests is the physi-

23

cian Joseph-Claude-Anthelme Récamier (1774-1852), who increased his renown in the eyes of his aristocratic patrons when he put his career on the line by refusing to take the oath of allegiance required of him by the new government. Although he had made his reputation in 1799 with his first book, on the treatment of hemorrhoids, the only book Récamier wrote after his fall from grace was probably more significant; it was a study of cholera, facilitated by the epidemic which raged in the year after the Revolution.

The fact that the text explicitly compares the Chevalier Ténèbre to cholera is, on the one hand, a wry acknowledgement of what de Quélen and Récamier did after the Revolution; on the other hand, it also recalls a key motif of Sue's *Le Juif Errant*, whose symbolic central character's arrival in Paris is followed by a cholera epidemic–a token of the curse he bears on behalf of all working men. Sue, as Féval knew very well, had been an enthusiastic supporter of the Revolution of 1848–with the result that he had been forced into exile after the coup of 1851. *Knightshade* is, therefore, a metaphorical transfiguration of the story of the end of the era in which it is set, embodying the idea that the end in question was merely recapitulating and reaffirming the end at which the *ancien régime* had already arrived once before, in 1789. It is the story of an end already foreshadowed, of a tale already old but still somehow unexpected, despite being told for the second time–and what formula could be more appropriate than Galland's to the telling of a tale of that ironic sort?

The fantastic elements of the story are carefully juxtaposed with real people in a real situation, further emphasizing its chimerical quality. Féval is not trying to pretend that the past really was supernatural; quite the reverse. He is saying that it was mortal, and that there is a tragedy intrinsic to mortality that applies to whole past eras as well as to the individuals that lived in them.

A note on the title of the translation may be appropriate, given that it is not conventionally literal. The name *Ténèbre* is very obviously derived from the French noun "*ténèbres*," which means "*darkness*." Although *ténèbres* is used as if it were a plural–one refers to "*les ténèbres*" rather than "*la ténèbre*"–no singular form exists, nor can it function as an adjective (the adjective is *ténèbreux* or *ténèbreuse*). The temptation to construe the suggested–as opposed to the literal–meaning of *Le Chevalier Ténèbre* as "*The Dark Knight*" ought, therefore, to be avoided; the suggestion is arguably more akin to "*Darkness the Knight*," and this is why only one of the two brothers Ténèbre is cited in the title, although they are inseparable within the plot. It is also worth noting that "*chevalier*" does not perform the same noun/adjective double function in French that "*cavalier*" does in both English and French, so the temptation to construe the title as "*Cavalier Darkness*" is also one best avoided.

Because the double meaning of Féval's title cannot be reproduced in English, I have had to choose between a literal rendition that could hardly avoid being awkward and an admittedly overloaded suggestive one. I believe that I have made the better choice, but readers of what follows will doubtless make up their own minds, just as they will make up their own minds about the propriety and significance of the manner in which the Chevalier Ténèbre's manipulation of his audience is mirrored and extended by Féval's manipulation of his.

When it commenced serialization in *Le Musée des Familles* in April 1860, the first installment of *Knightshade* was prefaced by the following note: "Simple advice to readers, especially female readers: do not begin this story before going to bed." This advertisement, like every other feature of the novel–including, most conspicuously, its title–carried a double meaning. It implied, on the one hand, that the story would be scary, but it also linked it more securely to the demand made of the mysterious Baron by the Bishop of Hermopolis that he should tell a story according to the Galland formula. For the benefit of modern readers, of course, the advice has to be reversed. The very best time to read a scary story is a dead of night, when one is likely to get the fullest possible benefit of its scariness–and the best time to test the irresistibility of a stand-in Scheherazade is exactly when the original tested her suspenseful skills: in opposition to the seductions of sleep.

Brian Stableford

Chapter I
One of Archbishop de Quélen's Soirées

Dinner had been taken at the Château de Conflans, the home of His Grace the Archbishop of Paris. It was not merely a priests' banquet; there were women present. Along the river bank on the road to Charenton, white dresses could be seen among the green lawns.

I don't know why that part of the Parisian countryside seems so sad. Are they not charming, those meadows where the Marne arrives to marry its waters with those of the Seine? Wine is gaiety, it is said; how is it that the ocean of wine that floods the town of Bercy does not enliven those heart-rending pastures in the slightest? Bacchus, whose praises are sung by our drunken poets, is there–can he not brighten up those mournful horizons? The Seine cannot contrive a smile while passing between them; the very trees seem sad. Ivry is sullen and sulky on one bank; on the other the park–which is so beautiful, in spite of the dismal pleasure-gardens on its edge, that its lawns should extend gloriously in the sunlight–is sulky and sullen behind its grey walls, at whose gate two sickly lions devoid of spirit or courage wrestle two boars which yawn as they defend themselves.

It is an exit. Parisian storytellers and chroniclers find the melancholy zone which starts at Charenton and extends as far as Bicêtre an ideal setting for their werewolves, brigands and phantoms. That flat country was a little less ugly in the past than it is today but it had a worse reputation in those days. As your aged uncles will tell you, nights thereabouts were full of horrors. Sabbaths were held–big ones–not far from the present site of Ivry railway station; the cemetery of the same name had not a single grave whose stone could keep it sealed, whether it was made of modern plaster or ancient cement. All the marble tombstones would raise themselves up at midnight, and whenever the darkness was briefly penetrated by the faint rays of the veiled moon, a long procession of the emergent dead could be seen to move slowly and silently upriver towards the monasteries of Vitry.

Archbishop de Quélen, as everyone knows, was not only a very eminent prelate but a perfect gentleman. His generosity towards the poor, an established historical fact, restrained his taste for luxurious and grandiose display, but his aristocratic heritage would not permit him to shut himself off from society. His receptions were carefully planned, especially those involving his closest friends. All shades of Royalist opinion would find an open and level field there, providing a lively opposition to the Restoration government in the very bosom of the House of Lords.

The events of our story took place in 1825; the Archbishop was then in his late forties, at the very height of his power as a primate of the Church of France and as a politician. In order that the glory surrounding him should lack for nothing, the Academy had also opened its doors to him.

This prelate–whose home some miserable wretches, who insulted the genuine people in taking the name of "the people," came to burn the day after the Revolution of July 1830–followed a well-known custom. He had made it a rule that after each of his receptions he would distribute to the poor a sum equal to the cost of his feast. I have heard it said by men who have never given anything to anyone that he would have done better to give twice as much and not receive visitors at all–well, perhaps. It would be necessary, in order to put together a jury capable of judging these good souls, to take immediate exception to all incapacity, all envy and all hatred. That would be hard work, and the preliminary hearing for the selection of the jury could take a long time. I said "perhaps" because although it is good to give, to do good is often better, because the eventual result is greater. The Lord Bishop de Quélen's feasts were productive, from the viewpoint of his benevolence. They rarely ended without misfortune having deducted its tithe from their serious and noble pleasures.

That was not all, however; Archbishop de Quélen also had another custom of which the Faubourg Saint-Germain and the court sometimes complained bitterly. He was a committed patron, always surrounded by an army of protégés, and he fought for these protégés with a courage that was as meritorious as it was redoubtable. His banquets were the peaceful tournaments where he broke lances on behalf of youth ardent to succeed, or old age eager to return after injury to the battle of life. I could name men in the highest places who would have good cause to remember the feasts of the Lord Bishop de Quélen.

It was an evening in September, in the same year that had seen the coronation of Charles X and the prodigious enthusiasm of Paris for the prince that Paris would, so soon afterwards, condemn to death in his absence. The weather was stormy and oppressively warm. Although night had begun to fall–dinner had been served at three o'clock, as was the fashion of the time–no one thought of going back indoors. The park was a welcome refuge from the torrid heat. The shade of the tall trees was fairly cool, and a light breeze blew fitfully from the low and ponderous river, trying to stir their leaves. The majority of the guests had come together again in the vast hall of verdure that was then the pride of the district, although the railway line to Lyon has since destroyed it. The Archbishop, who was by birth the Comte de Quélen, was originally of Breton descent; he belonged to the family that descended from the ducal houses of Aiguillon, Chaulnes and La Vauguyon; he was related to the Chateaubriants, the Rohans, the Dreuxes, the Guébriants, the La Bourdonnayes, the Coislins and the Goulaines. The gathering of all these names at the château, that evening, might have been a reunion of the general staff of François de Bretagne, or the court of Duchess Anne [1].

Such is the mysterious power of certain places that within that brilliant circle, in the glades where important theological questions had been debated from the days of François de Harlay, founder of the Château de Conflans, to those of the His Lordship de Talleyrand-Périgord [2], the predecessor of the present archbishop, the talk was all of brigands, werewolves and phantoms. To the great amusement of the women–and of the men too–marvellous tales of revenants were told, in the spirit of pure theatre. On the stage where the audience had reassembled, the narrators turned their tricks, as comedians say, pointing their fingers this way and that at the very fields that had served as scenery for their supernatural dramas.

The crowd, as always, included both believers and skeptics. Under the Restoration, the Faubourg Saint-

---

[1] (see Notes page 169.)

Germain had its little philosophical corner, and we know of more than one marquis of that era whose life was spent in imitation of Monsieur de Voltaire. In the matter of werewolves, incredulity is understandable, as it is with regard to phantoms, but brigands! That requires explanation. The skeptics on the subject of *brigandage* took refuge in a question of chronology. According to them, the day of the authentic brigand–the romanesque, picturesque, dramatic brigand–was done. The present era only had mere thieves–by way of recompense, however, the same skeptics contended that it did have a truly re-markable quantity of them.

Now, I defy you to take a ring of secular trees, about two or three hundred yards from an old château, and to place thereabouts, on a dark and stormy night, an assembly of thirty people discussing horrific or mystical subjects, without a kind of vague fear leaching into the conversational mix. I shall make a significant conces-sion, granting you two levels of incredulity–indeed, I will go even further, if you wish and grant you unanim-ity of skepticism, including the narrator himself, pro-vided that he is skilful, and I will still bet against you, so certain am I of what I say: the *frisson* of fear will arrive.

The *frisson* always arrives. It is not necessary, in the final analysis, for anyone in a circle affected by such a spirit to be a believer or victim of superstition. The frisson requires nothing but a powerful imagination. At the appointed moment, while the ordinarily timid re-strain a tremor, the strongly imaginative suffer nervous attacks and become faint. The "strongly imaginative" are typified by the brave boy who sings at the top of his voice in the darkness in order to allay his fears.

Among the more strongly imaginative members of the party on that evening at the Château de Conflans was a beautiful woman, very spiritual and very eloquent, whom we shall call the Princess de Montfort (because the actual names and titles of the persons in question must be protected; the Princess, having a leading role in our play, must be given the benefit of appearing incognito). She was there with her younger son, the Marquis de Lorgères, a tall, pale and handsome adolescent, who had been destined for the Church but had hesitated over his vocation. The Princess, who adored her younger son, affected a certain severity in her treatment of him, concealing her approval of the new route that he wished to take: the young marquis was ambitious to become a diplomat. The Princess was a slightly eccentric woman, but she was blessed with great intelligence and a good heart.

His Grace the Archbishop expressed no opinion on the matter of the supernatural or the persistence of *brigandage*, and seemed preoccupied with other matters. There were fors and againsts. His Lordship the Bishop Frayssinous of Hermopolis, who was then the Minister of Ecclesiastical Affairs, was an enthusiastic believer in the supernatural and had already recounted some fine tales. He was just beginning another when the Princess interrupted:

"It's becoming cold. Shouldn't we go back indoors?"

It would be inaccurate to speak of laughter bursting out. Laughter, especially of a mocking kind, does not "burst out" above a certain social level–but the Devil is everywhere and he never loses an opportunity. There was, in response to the words "it's becoming cold," a gentle murmur which tickled the ears of the Princess sufficiently to compel her to cry out: "Don't think that I'm afraid! Let's go!" The young and beautiful Comtesse de Maillé got up and came to drape a summer cloak over her aunt's shoulders.

"Auntie," she said, "let's tremble for a little longer–it's so nice!"

And everyone, in unison, cried: "Yes! Your story, My Lord Bishop!"

Instead of answering the general plea, the Bishop of Hermopolis remained silent for a moment. Then, in a restrained voice whose altered tone caused more than one heart to beat faster, he asked abruptly: "Are you not here, Monsieur von Altenheimer?"

There was another moment of silence. The moon displayed half her face between two storm-clouds that were as solid and heavy as slugs of lead. The Princess called her son to her side.

"Indeed I am," a deep baritone voice replied, profound and full of metallic vibrations. "I am here, My Lord."

The person who had spoken was unseen. His voice seemed to come from the trunk of a huge dead elm whose leafless branches took fantastic form in the sudden moonlight.

"Come closer, Baron, I beg you," the Bishop replied, "and relate to us, according to the Galland formula, one of those tales that you tell so well."

A man of tall and slender stature immediately moved into the middle of the circle. It seemed to the Princess, in the grip of her powerful imagination, that he had sprung from the earth, so sudden was his appearance. Nothing in the world could have renewed her determination to retreat to the château.

The light of the moon fell directly upon the newcomer, and it is a fact that everyone saw something extraordinary in him. That may also have been a result of the general predisposition. No one knew him; no one had seen him at dinner. He was doubtless one of those who had been invited purely for the after-dinner discussion; several other members of the audience were in the same situation. His costume, which was black from top to toe, was very formal, resembling that of the other laymen present. Why, then, use the word extraordinary? It was a mystery, quite inexplicable. Save for the pallor of his long Teutonic features, he was like all those who surrounded him, and yet the word was appropriate. The company was dumbstruck, as if a trapdoor had opened to allow the passage of a fantastic individual. The moon scarcely had time to illuminate him before it was hidden by a large cloud and obscurity enveloped him again.

"I am at His Lordship's disposal," said the baritone voice.

"That is most kind," replied the Bishop of Hermopolis, adding as he took the newcomer's hand: "Ladies, I have the honor of presenting to you the privy councilor Baron von Altenheimer, director general of the police of His Majesty the King of Wurtemburg...³" The privy councilor must have bowed, I suppose, but no one saw it.

"...And elder brother," the illustrious Bishop continued, "of Monsignor von Altenheimer, prelate of Rome, Chamberlain to Our Holy Father..."

"Here present," put in a tenor voice, as soft as a note from a flute. That tenor voice reassured the beautiful women a little.

"What kind of story does My Lord Bishop desire?" the baritone voice asked. "Phantoms or brigands? We have both of them in the Black Forest."

"Phantoms!" half the circle voted.

"Brigands!" opined the Princess, under the influence of her strong imagination.

The fearful, on the other hand, eager for a fine time of mortification by terror, demanded: "Vampires!"

Whereupon His Grace the Archbishop de Quélen, with a mildness in which a light note of irony was perceptible, said: "One could make an agreeable mixture out of all these good things."

"That's it! That's it!" cried the Bishop of Hermopolis, in the voice of a man who is certain of the virtue of what he has produced. "Baron, these ladies desire a tale to make their hair stand on end, in which there is a phantom, a brigand and a vampire all at the same time!"

"Hilarius," said the soft tenor voice, "The tale of the brothers Ténèbre is precisely that."

"Yes," the baritone replied, at the utmost depth of its range, "you're right, Benedict: the tale of the Ténèbre brothers!"

"The name is well-chosen!" murmured the Princess, suppressing a giggle while her hand closed convulsively upon the arm of her son, the Marquis de Lorgères.

"The name is not chosen at all!" replied the Monsignor, his tone a trifle piqued. "Everyone in Germany has heard of the Ténèbre brothers."

"And everyone in Paris will have heard of them soon," said the privy councilor quietly, as if he were speaking in spite of himself.

Even if the name had not been chosen for effect, one could nevertheless say that it was as appropriate as any that might have been invented. The circle drew closer. This was not included in the program of the soirée, which would culminate in a benefit concert, but it was worth ten times as much as the entire banquet. Chance gave to His Lordship's guests an unexpected performance, a delightful surprise–and, although no one could explain exactly why, it is certain that the hearts of our beautiful ladies were considerably stirred by emotion and alarm.

Baron von Altenheimer resumed an oratorical tone that served to emphasize his German accent. "Your excellencies, and most illustrious persons, my brother and I are strangers in the capital of France, and we are both charged with a difficult mission. We desire to be worthy of the generous welcome that has been extended to us, and of the protection that we have been promised. My brother Benedict will sing some traditional Westphalian songs for you this evening, and a few original Christmas ballads. I have a voice that is good enough for the chorus but not for solo performance, so I am glad to have found an opportunity to make myself equally agreeable. Historical legends and other traditional tales featuring the supernatural are so very abundant in our homeland that I would have had a thousand to choose from in attempting to satisfy your curiosity. I prefer, however, to set aside our popular tales and tell you a true story of the same kind, based on my personal experience and that of my brother. Here, a little while ago, I heard some very powerful people of both sexes discussing age-old controversies say: There are no more specters. A very illustrious lady exclaimed: There are no more authentic brigands; the times of Rob Roy, Schinderhannes, Zawn, Schubry, Mandrin and even Cartouche are gone. We no longer have anything but thieves [4]! I admit that we have an enormous number of thieves, but I am compelled to affirm that we also have brigands. Leaving aside the successors of Fra Diavolo [5] in southern Italy, Hungary, Bohemia and the southern provinces of Austria still produce bandits fully worthy of that name. On the other hand, specters continue to lift up the stones of their graves just as they did in the past: nothing changes in that sphere. I have seen vampires in the region of Belgrade and phantoms in our own cemetery at Tübingen."

We are relying here upon our memory, and we have made every effort to reproduce Baron von Altenheimer's preamble word for word. The manner of his delivery was remarkably well-suited to his style. To begin with, there was in both a depth of *naiveté*, which imparted an emphasis to certain expressions. On the surface, there were unequivocal signs of knowledge: a literary mixture of the philosophical and the scientific; the overall impression, however, was one of oratory pretension, with a distinct whiff of charlatanry, as serious as the black robe of a professor.

His Lordship the Bishop de Quélen leant towards the ear of his neighbor and said to him: "That's Germany [6]."

The judgement is not without profundity. That is Germany, indeed: that old wives' wisdom; that bourgeois philosophy; that naive predisposition to make a discourse of what Paillasse [7] called patter; all of it accompanied, supported and perhaps saved by a sort of nobility, which may deserve the name of truth. The ladies would not have made any such analysis, but the Baron's preface pleased them regardless. The session turned into a public lecture in the German manner, concerning phantoms and brigands–the two most frightful and interesting things in the world.

The propitious moon, as if to join the party, emerged in full from behind its cloud to muffle the dread that might have prevented us from paying full attention. The illuminated glade gained a sort of gaiety without losing its poetry.

The tall, black-clad German could be seen distinctly now, his two wide eyes shining in his long pale face. His younger brother, the monsignor, stood beside him; he was shorter and plumper, wearing a garment that was not quite a frock-coat and not quite a cassock, after the fashion of the priests of Rome.

The elder brother wore a badge of office as florid as that of any privy councilor in the tales of Hoffmann [8]. The younger wore no decoration at all, save for a long chain of polished steel, which passed around his neck above the dark collar of his coat and dangled by his right side. On the end of the chain was a rectangular object, also of polished steel, which seemed to contain a breviary or a missal.

All around them, the circle of listeners emerged from the shadows: heads handsome or venerable, foreheads furrowed, blonde tresses, avid eyes, mouths agape...

"Most illustrious friends," Baron von Altenheimer continued...

Chapter II
Chandor Castle

"In 1821, there was a Magyar family living in the ancient Chandor Castle near the banks of the river Tisza,
not far from the city of Szeged–which is some seven
leagues around and has eighty thousand inhabitants. All
Magyars are aristocrats, but these were princes of the
house of Baszin, whose founder had befriended Matthias
Corvinus, the Charlemagne of the Danube nations [9].

"Chrétien Baszin, Prince Jacobyi, possessed an immense fortune, evidence of which was met throughout
the land; he had thousands of peasant serfs, including
Serbs, Czechs, Croats and Walachians. His estate was as
big as a province and extended as far as that isle of vine-
yards surrounded by a sea of maize where the Turkeve
harvest the amber liquid of their royal vintages.

"The massive walls of Chandor Castle, situated on
the edge of an oak-forest, overlooked the Tisza. Its four
large thickset towers bulged at the top like the turbans of
the Turks who had constructed them in olden times.
From the tops of the towers one could see the minarets
of Szeged in the distance, beyond the vast cornfields. Its
pasturelands fed eight hundred horses and twice as many
cattle: proud Hungarian beasts with pearly hides and
widespread white horns. The prince was as generous as
he was magnificent: fifty places were always set at the
enormous square table that was placed every day when

the bell sounded noon on a silver dais in a cedarwood-paved courtyard beneath the open sky.

"You, ladies and gentleman, are the happy citizens of the most civilized nation on the globe, but you probably do not have an accurate idea of the aristocratic life in certain other countries that you call barbarian. There, we did not have–I say we because I have spent many years with the prince in Chandor Castle–all the refinements of your spotless, white and dainty French dinner services, and perhaps we lacked the fine delicacies of the portable luxury, if I may call it that, that you carry in your luggage on your tours of Europe, but we lived in a grand and luxurious style nevertheless, among all the proud display of absolute power.

"It is for such as they, the last high barons, that the purest juice of your Bordeaux grapes in carefully extracted; it is for them that the most piquant spirit of your champagnes is trapped. The American Indians, it is said, sell their gold for small quantities of whisky; you sell your nectars for small quantities of gold, and it is, alas, only rarely that a French gullet is permitted a taste of those astonishing ambrosias. To taste your wines you must go to Russia or the far shore of the Danube. Chevet sends his fresh vegetables and preserves, Lesage his pastries; we have everything that you have–and we have, in addition, the noble game of wild boars and your champagne whisked in the crushed pulp of our watermelons.

"Thus far, there is no hint of menace in my tale; but the sky is blue above our heads and the moon is bright–nevertheless, the storm is there, and it will break soon enough. Prince Jacobyi did not know the extent of his fortune. Once a month his stewards brought him their accounts, which he accumulated, unread, in his library.

Vast as it was, his library gradually became cluttered, its tiled floor hidden beneath untidy heaps of paper. Each month he signed, unread, a warrant addressed to his banker in Pest, in order to obtain money by means of a mortgage.

" 'Such as they would have to rob me prodigiously,' he would say, 'if they were ever to get to the bottom of my inheritance!' And when he looked at his daughter Lenore, a sweet-natured golden-haired angel, he would exclaim: 'I defy anyone to prevent this one from being the richest heiress for a hundred leagues around!'

"That was what he said, and truer words were never spoken by any man alive; but he had two stewards in his house and a banker in the city of Pest. As the proverb says, one steward is enough to devour an estate.

"Lenore was fourteen years old. It was already obvious that she was as beautiful as her mother, whose smiling portrait illuminated the house. Her life was solely devoted to learning; in those barbarian lands young women are highly and extensively educated. She had only one friend in the entire world: a girl of her own age—also a Magyar and an aristocrat, but poor—with whom she had been raised. Lenore had recently experienced the first tragedy of her life: Efflam, her companion, had left her to visit her father and mother, who lived near the border, not far from Belgrade.

"One evening, two Walachian gypsies arrived at the castle. They belonged to a wandering tribe that had camped in the banate of Timisoara on the other side of the Tisza. They had rowed across the river—which flows as fast as the Rhone and is three times as wide as the Seine, although it is only a tributary of the royal Danube. The night was just like this one, and I remember that the setting moon was continually appearing and disappear-

41

ing behind black clouds so thick that its gleam could not tint their fringes with silver. The tortuous mirror of the waters of the Tisza were soon to be plunged into the profoundest obscurity. The storm was in the southeast, the direction from which the menacing clouds were moving. The two wretches asked for hospitality.

"Lenore had been sad since the departure of Efflam, and the prince–who adored her–said to her: 'These people know how to juggle and do conjuring tricks. Would you like them to come in to entertain you?'

"Lenore shook her head languidly to signal her refusal–but when a servant said that the tribe had come from Belgrade, her eyes lit up.

" 'Bring them in,' she instructed.

"They were two brothers, the older still young, the younger very young indeed. They gave their names as Mikhael and Solim. Mikhael was the taller, and his features gave every evidence of his origin among those lost children of a forgotten civilization who are strangers in every nation of the world, having neither law nor God: the Egyptians of Scotland, the bohemians of France, the *gitanos* of Spain, the *zingari* of Italy. Solim, by contrast, had a pale fresh face, blue eyes and blond hair.

"The prince ordered them to entertain Lenore. Solim sang the strange melodies of the Moldavian lands, accompanying himself on his rounded guitar with two steel strings. Mikhael performed the dances of Yataghan, and both of them juggled with wine-glasses, bottles and knives.

"Lenore only yawned, and the prince made a gesture of dismissal.

" 'Hospodar [10],' said Mikhael, instead of obeying, 'wouldn't your daughter like to hear a good story?'

"His impudent eyes were fixed upon Lenore, who blushed and seemed ill-at-ease. The prince knitted his brows and opened his mouth to call for his servants, but the gentle voice of Lenore stopped him.

" 'Father,' she said, 'I would like to know...'

"Mikhael immediately took a step towards the girl, threw his cap upon the floor and knelt upon it, while Solim remained standing in the middle of the room, his eyes lowered and his arms crossed upon his breast. Mikhael reached out, demanding Lenore's hand, which she offered to him in spite of herself. He examined it minutely for a long time, speaking periodically in an unknown language. These words were addressed to Solim, who still stood motionless in the middle of the room; they seemed to make an extraordinary impression on him. His limbs trembled, the veins in his forehead swelled up, and the hair on his head shook. It was as if the pythoness of old were on her tripod.

"Mikhael had examined the hand, but it was Solim who played the oracle, saying: 'Hospodar! Woe is mine, who must cry woe! I see through the night, in the distance, the vampire Ange whose eyes are upon your daughter...'

"The prince burst out laughing, while Lenore grew pale.

" 'Are there still vampires?' cried the prince, who was still amused.

"Mikhael returned to stand beside his brother and put his hand over Solim's mouth. The prince's face clouded over. Thumping the table with his hand, he said: 'For my part, I want to know! And remember that the Chief Magistrate of Szeged would not trouble himself at all about a couple of miscreants suspended from the trees in my park!'

" 'Lord,' Mikhael replied slowly, 'you have enough servants to guard your daughter, and you owe us some recompense for having warned you.'

" 'Who is this vampire Ange?' asked Lenore, all a-tremble.

"Solim replied, while wiping the sweat from his brow: 'It is the younger of the Ténèbre brothers.'

" 'And who are the Ténèbre brothers, knave?' cried the prince.

" 'You have the right to abuse me, Lord,' Mikhael replied, drawing himself up to his full height. 'You are strong and I am weak. You also have the right to chase me out into the gathering storm and to have me beaten by your Slovaks, but I have no desire to tell you anything but the truth: the Ténèbre brothers are two of the dead.'

"Lenore huddled close to her father, while Solim repeated, as if he were an echo: 'Two of the dead!'

"The prince took his daughter in his arms and said: 'Explain yourselves.'

" 'Hospodar,' Mikhael began, 'are they not dead, and thoroughly dead, who have swayed in the wind for three days and three nights on the gallows? We wander ceaselessly, as you know, in search of the bread that never satisfies our accursed hunger. Between Itèbe and Semlin the gallows of Magnate Karolyi, the High Lieutenant of the Banate of Timisoara, is to be found [11]. We passed close by it on the twenty-seventh of October of last year, three days before the feast of All Hallows. There were two men hanging there, one large and one small. We stripped them bare, and went on our way.

"'On the first of November, as we returned towards Itèbe, heading for Belgrade, we found the two executed men again, still stripped bare, surrounded by a flock of crows. We made camp on the flat area between the gibbet and the Danube.

" 'At midnight, we were awakened by the sound of the crows, which were cawing plaintively. There was no moon, but there was another light, brighter and more vivid than moonlight. Where was it coming from? By means of that illumination we saw a huge cloud of fleeing crows. We saw, too, the gibbet, silhouetted in black against the strange aurora, with its two corpses slowly swinging.

" 'Two white horses with flowing manes ran right past us, bearing neither bridle nor saddle; they glided like arrows, but we heard not the slightest sound of their hoofbeats. They both halted beneath the gallows, one beneath the taller hanged man, the other beneath the shorter. We saw the four limbs of the executed men move, separating one from another.

" 'A sudden glare ripped through the cold November clouds like summer lightning; the two gallows-ropes broke at exactly the same moment and the two cadavers fell as one, legs apart, on to the two horses, which galloped away to the sound of a thunderclap...'

" 'See how feverishly my poor, dear Lenore is shivering,' said the prince. 'Take your tall stories to hell with you!'

"Solim lowered his arms, murmuring: 'My brother Mikhael has told the truth.'

"And Lenore, whose pretty white teeth were chattering, said: 'They are amusing me, Father–let them go on.'

" 'At Itèbe,' Mikhael continued, 'we asked the names of the two criminals, and were told that they were the Ténèbre brothers: Ténèbre the bandit and Ténèbre the vampire. Now, in the middle of the Great Hungarian

Plain there are two graves that you can see for your-selves, one large and one small. Each is covered by a black stone, both of which carry inscriptions in the French language: on the larger one. Jean Ténèbre, *Chevalier*; on the smaller, Ange Ténèbre, *Prêtre*. Edu-cated men say that they are the tombs of two French no-blemen who came with many others to help the voivode John Hunyadi [12] defend Christendom against the Turks four hundred years ago. Men who are not educated af-firm that for four centuries there has lain beneath these marble slabs an oupire and a vampire: one an eater of human flesh, the other a drinker of human blood.

" 'Hospodar, one thing is certain! On many occa-sions, during the four hundred years, those graves have opened, to the terror and the horror of the surrounding country. Sometimes, two corpses were found beneath the stones, one tall and one short, which gave every indica-tion of recent death: eyes open and shining, blood liquid in the veins, tongues moist and lips red. At other times, the open graves displayed nothing but their emptiness: two black cavities from which the odor of death emerged. It is certain, moreover, that many attempts have been made to destroy these graves: the marble slabs have been broken, the rubble dispersed, the ground lev-eled–and invariably, when some time has passed, the two black stones resurface beneath the grass or the corn, intact once again, bearing the same funerary inscriptions.

" 'Lastly, it is certain–as the registers of the courts testify–that within the last twenty years alone, the broth-ers Ténèbre have been hanged in a dozen different places in Hungary, and seven times impaled in Turkish terri-tory.

" 'But supernatural occurrences make little impact, unless they happened in the recent past. It is a story of

46

the recent past that I want to tell you now. After having wandered for six months in the Turkish lands and traversed part of Serbia, our tribe returned towards Belgrade and camped once again on the banks of the Danube, below Semendria [13].

" 'At midnight, those of our kin who were keeping watch perceived two lights moving slowly downstream on the surface of the river. They went to investigate, and found two leather bags, one large and one small, drifting in the current, each one bearing a lamp and a placard headed The Pasha's Justice. The placard attached to the larger bag also bore the name Jean Ténèbre; that of the smaller, the name Ange Ténèbre.

" 'These two cadavers had been set afloat because the treasury of Belgrade had been looted three days previously and the daughter of the learned treasurer had been found dead in her bed, as white as an alabaster statue. We heard of the theft and the murder later–but when our sentinel came to wake us, we saw a long black boat that drifted by itself in the current with no one to steer it. The black boat came abreast of the two dying lights and, a moment later, had turned against the current as swiftly as a bird in flight, and was steered upriver by two men, one tall and one short.

" 'We arrived on the following day–the day beginning this very week–at the gates of the town of Petrovaradin in Slavonia...'

" 'Where my dear Efflam is, father,' murmured Lenore, offering her face to her father's kiss.

" 'It was morning,' Mikhael continued. "We pitched our tents in the place reserved for our tribes, under the ramparts of the town between the cemetery and the black ditch watered by the river Drave, into which the bodies of dead animals and executed criminals are

47

carelessly thrown. We thought that there must be a festival in the town, because a great throng of peasants was pressing at the gates. When we were allowed to enter,we found that the festival was a public execution by the sword. On the scaffold, we saw two condemned men, one tall and one short. And two names were on everyone's lips: the brothers Ténèbre! Hospodar, the heads fell: I saw it with my own eyes...'

" 'The heads fell,' Solim repeated, 'and they rolled across the planks of the scaffold.'

" 'And we returned to the camp,' continued Mikhael, 'behind the cart which carried the executioner's work. The two heads and the two bodies were thrown into the ditch in front of us while, on the far side of our tents, a poor child of fifteen years was carried to the cemetery.'

" 'Her name! The name of the dead girl!' cried Lenore, as if she had been seized by a heart-rending presentiment.

" 'Efflam,' replied Mikhael.

" 'Efflam!' repeated Solim, with lowered eyes and flared nostrils.

"Lenore put both hands to her breast and collapsed, deprived of her senses, into her father's arms..."

Baron von Altenheimer paused at this point, and Monsignor Benedict took the opportunity to say, in a very soft voice: "I admire the memory of my dear brother the privy councilor. While he was speaking, it seemed to me that he could still hear that rogue the Chevalier Ténèbre–for no one here can have failed to divine that Mikhael, the pretended gypsy, Mikhael the Romany, was none other than the elder of the brothers Ténèbre."

Chapter III
A Wedding in Venice

The Princess much preferred this tale to others, which might have featured French brigands or indigenous phantoms. The overall impression produced on us by a tale will, it must be admitted, depend on the involuntary response of the listeners themselves. This remark is particularly true with respect to fictions calculated to produce fear. No legend or fantastic tale will ever produce in a Parisian drawing-room the shivers that will find you out by a huge log fire, gathered around the enormous fireplace of an ancient château. Specters no longer come into Paris, as everyone knows. Listeners can be amused, but not frightened–but in cases like the present one, amusement can only be truly or fully obtained in being frightened.

Baron von Altenheimer's tale seemed curious, and that was all. All that it had contrived in its audience was that level of emotion that is so easily produced in the theatre, as soon as the curtain rises half-way and some unknown person crosses the darkened stage with his hat tilted over his eyes. Fear no longer exists. Parisians cannot be frightened–not top drawer Parisians, at any rate–by the vampires of the Drave and French cavaliers interred for four hundred years in the Great Hungarian Plain!

The Princess was so completely cured of her terror that she looked at her son the Marquis and laughed. She found that he was very pale, and was on the point of asking him whether he could take such solemn nonsense seriously–but everyone seems pale by moonlight. The Princess let go of the Marquis; she had no further need of his bodily protection.

"Monsieur le Baron," said the benevolent and courteous Archbishop of Paris, "we did not expect such good fortune. Permit me to thank the Bishop of Hermopolis for all the pleasure that you have given us this evening."

The audience chorused its approval. In high society, as our readers well know, the bravos are always polite, and triumphs are a thousand times sweeter.

But the Bishop of Hermopolis was not content. He had hoped for more than this. One expects a great deal from the virtuosos one has produced. Several signs of impatience had escaped His Lordship. "It must be admitted," he said, in his rich southern accent, "that Monsignor von Altenheimer has favored us with an unfortunate revelation! How can you expect us to be interested in the story, now that we know how it ends?"

"Does Your Excellency really know how it will end?" asked the hollow voice of the Baron.

That single sentence was sufficient to make everyone pay attention. The Bishop, already modifying his tone, said: "Seeing that we know that the two bohemians are none other than Jean and Ange Ténèbre in person, young Lenore will surely be devoured..."

"By no means!" cried the Princess, all her courage evaporating. "I certainly hope that we shall be able to save her... isn't that so, Monsieur le Baron?"

The privy councilor to His Majesty the King of Wurtemburg offered a respectful bow to the whole audience, and directed more specific ones at the Minister and the Princess. By the rays of the moon, one could see a satisfied expression upon his long face. He took from his pocket a big golden box, embellished with large sparkling diamonds, which sent scintillating reflections in all directions.

"Noble ladies and gentlemen," he replied soberly, playing with his royal snuff-box–which looked for all the world like a handful of pure light–"my brother Benedict has done no wrong. Nor has he, as His Excellency appears to believe, given away the punch-line of the joke–God grant that it were, in fact, a joke! Unhappily, in telling tales like these one can disdain such cleverness. There is no need to manage with due care the petty effects and little surprises that storytellers usually employ. I will give you further proof of this by telling you straight away that the Ténèbre brothers are now in Paris, and that I have come here in pursuit of them, at my own risk and peril."

This time, the majority of the audience-members started violently, while the remainder pricked up their ears. The Bishop of Hermopolis, who stubbornly insisted on seeing the matter from an artistic viewpoint, clapped his hands and cried bravo. The Princess recalled her son, the Marquis de Lorgères, to her side.

"That's some joke," she murmured.

Baron von Altenheimer slowly inhaled a pinch of snuff, then–just as slowly–he wiped the back of his hand on his black coat. It must be admitted that such a gesture is more effective at the *Comédie Française*; it really requires a frill. Even so, it wasn't bad, for a Westphalian.

"Now!" the Baron continued, in a deliberate tone. "I shall proceed as swiftly as I can to the matter of the crown jewels of Wurtemburg. Consider, noble ladies, the fact that in the 19th century, we live our lives surrounded by prodigious events that, for some reason, we neither see nor deny. Personally, I am a believer, because I have learned the truth to my cost. I believe in the Chevalier Ténèbre, the most audacious, the most improbable, the most authentically diabolical brigand who ever lived; I believe in Ange Ténèbre, the vampire. I have seen the pale remains of his victims, from which not a drop of blood could be recovered.

"What is the exact nature of beings like these, and where do they fit into the known categories of God's Creation? I don't know. A theory that could accommodate such monstrosities would have to extend much further than ordinary moral failings or deviations from the common mold. There must be prodigies within the order of created beings that are immediately superior to mankind and, in consequence, unknown to mankind. Seeing that the fraction of the work of God that is visible and tangible to us presents anomalies–since we encounter in our streets hunchbacks, hare-lips and idiots–it may be that death itself, or the mechanical organization of life, if you prefer, is similarly subject to deviations and *dérangements*. It may be that the clay of which we are formed is occasionally treated with other and more powerful reagents..."

"Monsieur Privy Councilor... brother," Monsignor Benedict interrupted at this point, "I beg you to drop this subject, lest you become enmeshed in the toils of sinful materialism."

This was said with gentle severity. Baron von Altenheimer extended his hand to his younger sibling and said: "I beg your pardon, brother."

"It could be explained, up to a point," Monsignor Frayssinous put in, "without any recourse to materialistic philosophy..."

"Of course, Excellency, of course," the Baron interrupted respectfully, "but it's entirely my concern. I have my reasons for believing, so I believe; that's quite sufficient. An objection of a different order has been put forward, which appears to me more serious, because it challenges my conduct. The question needs to be put to me: if you are a believer, as you affirm, how is it possible that you would compromise your good character by such vain speculations? You accept the reality of these two creatures of popular superstition, and you commit yourself to their pursuit! Why? To kill them, even though they are immortal? Ladies and gentlemen, in our German universities we call this a disputation. I believe that these creatures have existed for four centuries and more..."

At this point, the Baron was interrupted by a murmur mingled with a certain amount of politely-muffled laughter.

"He is superb," the Bishop of Hermopolis said, in a low voice. "He sets out these follies with such magnificent sang-froid."

"...For four centuries and more," repeated Baron von Altenheimer. "That is my utterly firm and very well-established opinion–but I do not believe that they are immortal. Tradition is definite upon this point. No oupire or vampire can resist combustion. As it will probably fall to me to defend France, I propose to put this theory–advocated by all ancient authors–to the test by taking the

53

miscreants to Stuttgart, where they will be carefully burned, after which their ashes will be divided into small portions and transported in several different directions before they are scattered on the ground. If they rise again, after that, then will be the time to say that the privy councilor, Baron von Altenheimer, is nothing but a poor head without a brain!"

There were some in the audience who thought that the tall German gentleman with the *basso-profundo* voice was simply and deplorably mad. Others supposed that he was joking. The remainder, among whose ranks was the Princess, were inclined to concede that his was a rather ingenious method of exterminating oupires, vampires and the like.

"You will not be surprised to know," Baron von Altenheimer continued, "that misfortune was not long arriving in the house of Prince Jacobyi. His daughter was carried off that very same night. How vast the sums were that the brothers Ténèbre had appropriated by theft is unknown—but it is certain that they loved money. Some said that they had buried fabulous treasures in various different places in southern Germany.

"Prince Jacobyi was advised that his daughter Lenore would be returned safe and sound on payment of a ransom of half a million florins, but he was warned that if he made the slightest effort to recover her by force, or by recourse to the law, the child would be lost to him forever.

"He did not hesitate. Forty-eight hours later, he had the twelve hundred thousand francs—and Lenore, safe and sound, as promised, slept in her own bed that night. But it happened that the Chevalier Ténèbre and his brother Ange, the vampire, were not the only bandits who had dealings with the Magnate: his two stewards and his banker in Pest were also vampires, after their own fashion. They had been mining his fortune for a long time, and the loan of five hundred thousand florins caused an explosion.

"All his creditors demanded settlement of their mortgages at the same time, and in the full amount. The Chandor domain was put up for public auction. It was not so much an estate as a country; even in the depths of Hungary it was worth more than two million *louis*. The prince, once the sale was made, had only just enough to pay off his debts–but the two stewards and the banker in Pest were now as rich as lords.

"The Prince became an expatriate. He may be in England, or Italy, or perhaps in France. He lives, it is said, on what his daughter earns...

"My lords, the night would be entirely gone and the new day born before I could complete a detailed account of the horrors with which the voice of the public has charged the brothers Ténèbre. Their name, if spoken aloud in the regions through which the Danube flows, will not only put women and children to flight but strong men. Captain, or Chevalier Ténèbre, as he is variously known, has fought pitched battles against entire troops of Austrians and Turks; he has plundered tax-collectors and routed their protective escorts ten times over. Ange, his brother, is no soldier, but don't think him any less dangerous for that. He is a master of disguise, well able to play any role; the captain and he are on an absolutely equal footing. They amass their fortune ceaselessly, and I have often heard it said in Hungary, not only by the common people but in the reception-rooms of the Arch-duke in the Imperial Palace at Ofen, that if there were a kingdom for sale, the brothers Ténèbre would be kings.

"Last year in Venice, at the beginning of spring, the entire city was celebrating the marriage of the young Comtesse Barberini, the god-daughter of Her Royal and Imperial Majesty, to the scion of the Policeni family: it was the reunion of two of the greatest Lombardo-Venetian fortunes and from the dawn of the day the city wore the face of public celebration [14]. The poor people of Venice knew Pia Barberini as an angel of charity. It was said that Andrea Policeni–formerly a spirited young man, a king of patrician pleasures, the last of those mysterious Romans who slid under the Rialto in former times, behind the curtains of so many gondolas, when moonlight blanched the palace of the marble Venus risen from the crest of the wave–had divested himself of the dark mantle of the adventurer, cast it away and become a saint at her behest.

"I was in Venice, my lords, not on any political mission on this occasion, but merely to embrace my beloved brother, who was enrolled in the army of God, stationed in Rome with the Holy Father. Venice is halfway between Stuttgart and the Eternal City..."

As if each of the two brothers had yielded to an irresistible impulse of tenderness, their hands sought and clasped one another. The audience approved; the gesture was greeted with softened expressions, as a demonstration of the beautiful love that flourishes in families.

"We each made a journey, to meet one another at the half-way point," Baron von Altenheimer continued, in a slightly emotional voice. "At the wedding, in which we assisted, there were representatives of all the aristocracies in the world–but there were two strangers, in particular, who excited the curiosity of the entire city: John Stuart, Earl of Glasgow, the son of the pretender Charles Edward Stuart–and, in consequence, the legitimate heir to the English throne–and his younger brother Charles, the Duke of Richmond.

"The common opinion, to tell the truth, holds that the last Stuart died in Rome without issue; but even in Rome, as my brother Benedict can assure you, many eminent persons reserve doubts in that regard. The pretender, who had lived in fear of the combined intrigues of the House of Brunswick and his own brother, Henry Stuart, Cardinal Duke of York, had contracted a secret marriage and concealed the birth of his son, the supreme hope of a dynasty threatened on all sides [15]. The Earl of Glasgow was in possession of papers of the utmost importance. Certain titles, emanating from sources so respectable that to persist in doubting them is almost sacrilege, become unbelievable. The majority of the noblemen of Venice addressed the Earl of Glasgow as 'Majesty'.

"There was, moreover, the evidence of two particularly handsome faces–and, one might almost say, historic heads. John Stuart, who was a tall man, had a long and bilious face as similar to his father's as two drops of water on his coat of arms. His younger brother, by virtue of his curly blond hair and the delicate cut of his features, might easily have been mistaken for the subject of Van Dyck's portrait of Charles I–especially given his stature, for Charles was as short as his namesake.

"In the ancestral hall of the Barberini Palace there was a table of blue porphyry, supported by four massive silver feet. All the gems to be worn at the wedding had been assembled there; it was a jewel-case that a queen would have envied.

"There were the diamonds to be worn by the present Comtesse Policeni, who was a Howard, like the fifth wife of King Bluebeard, Henry VIII of England; those of the grandmother, Rose Gritti, and the great-grandmother, Ann Gradenigo; the ruby necklace in which Phébus of Lusignan had married Catherine Pépoli; the diadem of Catherine Cornaro, her mother, the Queen of Cyprus; and the sapphire *rivière* of Tranquille Paléologue, the wife of the last doge but one–and all of that on the bridegroom's side.

"On the bride's side could be seen the solitaire known as the Montserrat; the rose-cut diamond that the Dukes of Austria had carried in their crown; the seven brilliants of Pallas Comnène–the Pleiades; the bracelets of Antonia Doria of Genoa, who became the wife of Nicolas Barberini in the denouement of that eternal drama whose principal roles are Romeo and Juliet; the ring of Cardinal Frégose–and outshining all that marvelous finery–the wedding-present sent to his god-daughter by His Majesty the Emperor of Austria.

One touching incident occurred that can be told in a few words: the king without a crown, that heir to such misfortune and such grandeur, the Earl of Glasgow, advanced towards the porphyry table, laden with all these treasures, and asked for permission to throw upon it a simple string of pearls that had been worn by the unfortunate Mary, Queen of Scots. I can still see his venerable figure and the nobly ingenuous air of his young brother, as the affianced couple offered their thanks to him.

"And I swear, on my honor, that I did not begin to recognize in them the two sordid gypsies of Chandor Castle...!"

There arose in the circle of listeners such a murmur of astonishment that the Baron's words were literally cut off.

"Bravo! Bravo! *Bravissimo!*" cried the Bishop of Hermopolis. "That's what I call, for the sake of delicacy, a sudden reversal of fortune!"

"What?" said His Grace the Archbishop de Quélen. "That's too bad...!"

"I've guessed it," murmured the Princess. "In placing the false pearls on the porphyry table, the King of England slipped some beautiful diamond up his sleeve..."

Baron von Altenheimer offered her a dignified bow, and replied: "Beautiful lady, nothing escapes the perspicacity of the French. Except that the Chevalier Ténèbre did not perform his conjuring trick with all the world looking on, nor were the pearls false–for, that very night, he took them back, along with everything else that was on the porphyry table.

"What?" the cry went up. "All of them?

"All of them," confirmed the soft voice of the Monsignor. "Including the silver legs of the table."

Chapter IV
Baron von Altenheimer

The windows of the château, visible between the trees, were illuminated one by one. The final preparations were being made for the Archbishop's charitable distribution.

"We shall soon be interrupted, Baron," said the Bishop of Hermopolis, "but in the meantime, the ladies would dearly like to hear the end of your story."

"In other words, Your Lordship, you want me to cut it short," replied the King of Wurtemburg's privy councilor. "Well, in the first place, I am at the disposal of Your Excellency, and that of His Grace and all the other eminent persons who have done me the honor of listening to me–and in the second, I really do have only a little left to tell.

"I have not yet told you that the family of King Wilhelm, my master, is the most numerous surrounding any throne in Europe [16]. His Majesty has four children by his two marriages; his very illustrious son, likewise has four children; his five very respectable uncles have an even greater wealth of descendants, and such an assortment of children, grandchildren, sons-in-law and daughters-in-law, that the five collateral branches boast no less than fifty princely heads. God, the protector of France, also seems to concern himself a little with the dynasty of Wurtemburg.

"Now, all this notwithstanding, until 1823 King Wilhelm did not have a direct heir of the male sex. There was, in consequence, great joy in Wurtemburg when, on the sixth of March, the birth of a prince royal was announced, who was privately baptized, according to the rites of the Lutheran church, Charles Frederick Alexander. The King wanted to postpone the definitive baptism ceremony, in order to express the full extent of his gladness, and so that all the friends of the court might gather for a feast that would be both a public and a family celebration.

"There is no time to contrive any petty surprises, and in any case, after everything that had gone before everyone will be able to guess that the Ténèbre brothers came to the feast–but under what pretext, and in what form?

"I beg you, my dear lords and ladies, not to gauge these two truly prodigious beings according to the measure of your timid impostors, your bird-brained brigands or those phantoms whose puerile roles are restricted to the gratuitous terrorization of female feebleness and the poltroonery of little children. My judgement, which I have not sought to hide from you, is that we are faced here with the supernatural, employing means which are beyond our comprehension to satisfy two purely human passions: Avarice and Lust. Interred beneath those two black stones, covering the two graves on the Great Hungarian Plain, are not two corpses but two deadly sins, incarnate since the beginning of the world...in other places, there must be other marble slabs covering those other vampires which are always dead and yet always alive: Ambition, Wrath, Hatred, Dishonesty and Pride.

"You, who are amazed by the petty comedy played out by your Comte Pontis de Sainte-Helène, should not be tempted to make comparisons. Don't say that there are difficulties, or impossibilities, in my story–or anything else that might be masked by that loose term, implausibility, which is the protestation of minds that are too narrow against truths that are too broad.

"Yes, certainly, there were difficulties involved in entering that court, to mingle with the princes and princesses whose alliances embraced all Europe like a familial net. Yes, certainly, there were what the vulgar call impossibilities standing in the way of their presentation, under some royal name–and how else could they present themselves?–in that palace teeming with the guests and friends of all the real kings. Anyway, the brothers Ténèbre, as you would expect, chose their disguises and their roles with great care.

"This was not an occasion of the ingenuous phantasmagoria of Venice. Wurtemburg does not treat fallen royalty with such religious chivalry; it is a new and pragmatic realm, which has no fear of alloying its dynastic blood with that man who became your Emperor– and who, a mere four years ago, paid with his death on a desert island for the magical splendor of his victories. What was required here was, if you will permit me to express it thus, a solid emanation of an extant power. The occasion required someone living, not dead; it required, in a word, a personage that all the princes and all the princesses could call cousin, without creating a diplomatic incident or starting a war–a representative of a peaceful and relatively weak state.

"Where could that state be found? Not Russia, from which had come the late Queen, the daughter of Paul I, and whose armies were commanded by Prince Alexander, the King's uncle; nor Prussia, where Prince Auguste, the nephew of the King, served in the guards;

nor Austria, where Princess Marie, the cousin of the King, bore the title of Archduchess; nor any part of Germany, where Nassau, Saxe-Altembourg, Bade, Stolberg, Waldeck, Hohenloe, Tour-et-Taxis were all sons-in-law or fathers-in-law; nor the Netherlands, where a betrothal had already been secured between the heir to the throne and Princess Sophie, who was still in her cradle; nor England, where Duke Louis, the father of the actual Queen, lived; nor even France, the adopted fatherland of Duke Frederick Philip. Where, then?

"There is a troubled land, one of the greatest in history, but which seems in our modern epoch to be hiding behind its mountainous wall, ashamed of its decadence. Germany no longer knows Spain, now that the house of Austria has ended its reign in Madrid. The noise of your last war, the heroism of your princes and your soldiers at the Trocadero [17], reached us as a muffled echo, too distant to be heard. Spain is a China in the middle of Europe—but you know what effect that the ambassadors of India had on the court of Louis XIV; a literal Chinese ambassador would have caused a stir throughout Europe. At the baptism of our prince royal, no one paid any attention to the son of the Spanish *infanta*.

"Were there, then, no official diplomatic links between Spain and Wurtemburg? Yes, there were—there was still a Spanish *chargé d'affaires* in Stuttgart, but he was tricked into becoming an accessory. Notes were exchanged between Madrid and Stuttgart; it was my responsibility to look at them, and I looked at them. I am not particularly intimate with most of that which surrounds me but I am, after all, a learned man; in my own country I am an accredited savant. I hold doctoral diplomas from four universities. My sight is good, my health has not deteriorated under the strain of mental labor, I am perfectly sane–and yet those documents seemed authentic to me!

"I am not afraid to say it: it was a veritable miracle! Anyone who has been admitted into a chancellery, whether by the humble door that I use or by that which opens to the knocking of Your Excellencies, knows what a mountain of impossibilities–I will use the word, this time–must be climbed in order to create false diplomatic correspondence. Each such dispatch passes through a hundred hands that must be corrupted, and before a hundred eyes that must be blinded; but the correspondence was manufactured. I have in my files here in Paris a letter signed by King Ferdinand, but written by the Chevalier Ténèbre or by Ange Ténèbre the vampire!

"That's not all, however. The court at Wurtemburg had issued real and authentic notes; the court of Spain had responded, that much is certain. Add the suppression of the real documents to the creation of the false ones and your minds may boggle at their leisure–for that, I repeat, is a miracle.

"What remains to be told re-enters the category of ordinary prestidigitation. Once the two creatures had been able to trick me, acting and speaking as they did before me–who has paid so dearly for their acquaintance–it was merely a question of artfulness. It must be admitted that they had had all the time in the world to become accomplished impostors and admirable comedians. But those papers...!"

Baron von Altenheimer fell silent, as if his retrospective astonishment had choked him, and Monsignor Benedict sighed as he shook his blond head. "Ah! Don't you see... the papers! The papers! There is the miracle!"

Archbishop de Quélen leaned over to whisper into the ear of the Bishop of Hermopolis. "Well, it's stunning, I must admit... but it's only an audacious phantasmagoria, isn't it?"

"It's the truth," Bishop Frayssinous replied. "The pure truth! I have seen the Baron's own letters of credit, in the company of the prefect of police. He is highly respected at court. Besides, there's his brother–Chamberlain to His Holiness...

"But how is it," murmured the Archbishop, "that we have never heard talk of any of this?"

"It only happened a few days ago, Your Grace! The baptism of the Prince Royal of Wurtemburg took place at the end of August, and September has just begun."

"It was exactly a fortnight ago," said the Baron, who appeared to have fully recovered his composure. "All Stuttgart took part in the celebration, whose like had never been seen in our homeland. Fifty princes and princesses of the German and Northern courts were received at the castle–who, together with the army of princes and princesses related by blood, formed a veritable royal crowd. His Majesty said, joyfully: 'I have waited two and a half years, but it is a complete success. There is not a single fairy missing from my son's cradle!'

"He certainly appreciated how much he owed to the courtesy of the states of Germany and the North, but that which flattered him even more was the unexpected tribute from the South; what made his success complete was the presence of Don François de Paule, *Infante* of Spain, and his august companion, Louise-Charlotte de Bourbon, daughter of François I, King of Sicily.

"The *Infante* was a man of twenty-three years, dark-skinned but seeming not a day older than his ostensible age. It would have taken a sorcerer to detect any trace of resemblance between that bold and taciturn young man and the pretended heir to the royal privilege of the Stuarts, a stiff and desiccated old man whose ravaged features were already crowned with white hair. As for the *Infanta* Louise-Charlotte, we all knew that she was born in 1804, and was in consequence twenty-one years of age–and noble, gracious and charming! The Chevalier Ténèbre could pass for the king of actors, but there is no greater comedian than brother Ange: that is a magician who could make you see the sun at midnight!

"It was the brothers Ténèbre, and their brilliant retinue was probably the same gypsy band that camped on the far bank of the Tisza in full view of Chandor Castle. And that royal farce–which, it must be said, was probably unique in the annals of the world–was paraded for three full days before the assembled houses of Europe!

"It was the brothers Ténèbre! The denouement you already know, in part: the crown jewels of Wurtemburg disappeared during the second day. On the third day, an angelic child died, the daughter of Chancellor Reinhardt, who had been placed with the infanta in the capacity of maid-of-honor. That same day there was a general clear-out so audacious that the astonishment which seemed exhausted was reborn. Everything had gone: the jeweled ornaments of the princes and princesses alike.

"The *Infante* and the *Infanta* had done a great deal of dancing that evening. As midnight approached, Monsieur Metternich [18], whose sister is the King's aunt, asked the Archduchess Marie, the older sister of the Queen, what had become of the eagle modeled in diamonds that she normally wore at her throat. The Archduchess searched and, while searching, said to Monsieur Metternich in her turn: 'Prince, where is your Golden

Fleece necklace? Where is your Annunciation string? Where is your Danish brooch?' An immediate outcry went up, everyone perceiving at the same time that they had been robbed. The King–the King himself–had been stripped of the emblems of his identity! The doors of the palace were shut, but it was too late. The *Infante*, the *Infanta* and their retinue had already gone, carrying booty whose worth could not be estimated at less than a million gold crowns."

"At the very least," Monsignor Benedict added, equably.

A noise of carriage-wheels on the roadway, coming towards Conflans, was heard. The wind, which had begun to blow in gusts, carried vague sounds along the brilliantly-illuminated side of the château: fugitive instrumental notes groping in search of harmony. The Archbishop of Paris gave the signal to return, saying: "We can't be late arriving at our little concert!"

Everyone immediately stood up. The sensation of terror was utterly dispelled, for the very simple reason that the most recent episodes narrated by the baron had no trace of the diverse emotions that had previously agitated the assembly. The Venetian tale had been set in broad daylight; the adventure in Stuttgart had taken place by the bright light of a thousand candles; there had been no further return to the kind of dark and mysteriously moonlit night that surrounded the Archbishop's guests. Baron von Altenheimer's vampires and brigands had taken on the character of a comic opera.

The Princess took the arm of her son and bodyguard, the young Marquis de Lorgères. Pleased with herself because she was no longer trembling, she had just opened her mouth to reproach Baron von Altenheimer because she had not been sufficiently frightened, when she saw two eyes fixed upon her. They had that particular gleam that the eyes of animals of the feline genus take on in the darkness.

Madame de Montfort was an intelligent person, who knew perfectly well that vampires rarely interest themselves in princesses of a certain age; nevertheless, the gaze startled her. It belonged to Monsignor Benedict, who pointed a white and delicate finger, on which a magnificent solitaire sparkled, at the wide lawn in front of the château and said in a honeyed voice: "I would like to point out to Madame the Princess how easily even the simplest things can be reinvested with genuinely fantastic aspects by darkness."

In the middle of the lawn, a white object could be seen, which was moving slowly, cutting across the dark expanse of grass. It was a woman, but the way in which the diffuse rays of the moon fell upon her billowing dress really did give her the appearance of a ghost. She glided through the dark obscurity of the park like a hazy apparition. The arm of the young Marquis trembled beneath his mother's.

"Gaston! What is it?" she cried. "Are you trying to frighten me as well?"

"The wind is chilly," Gaston mumbled.

At that moment, the Archbishop said; "Do you see that phantom? It is my charming and angelic *protégée* Mademoiselle d'Arnheim, who will perform some beautiful classic masterpieces by the German masters for us. Ladies, I recommend her to you with all my heart, for she is a Christian Antigone who supports her father in his old age. The Opera is richer than we are, and has offered to pay two thousand *louis* a year for her unparalleled voice and admirable delivery. Mademoiselle d'Arnheim, who comes from a good family and is as pious as a prayer, would rather remain poor than risk her soul for gold; she is content to give lessons. I have promised to help her and would be very grateful to anyone who would like to second me in that good work."

The white form had disappeared behind the trees lining the avenue.

"Gaston," said the Princess, "you must go to see Monsieur Récamier about the beating of your heart. I can feel it against my arm; it's a veritable palpitation."

Baron von Altenheimer had drawn nearer to the Archbishop. "My Lord," he said, after a respectful hesitation, "perhaps I do not understand the French language well enough to express things very delicately. I am rich. Would it be possible for me do something, via Your Lordship, for the young lady who has the honor to be your *protégée*?" As he spoke, he took a pocket-book from inside his coat. The Archbishop looked at him and reached out a hand; it was only to clasp his, for he murmured: "Monsieur le Baron, you are a good-hearted man!" The Baron, however, pretending to have misunderstood him, deposited the wallet in the Archbishop's hand, bowed in an exaggerated fashion and disappeared into the crowd of guests.

The Princess came to a sudden halt at the foot of the steps and said to her son: "Gaston, I think I have left Madame de Maillé's cloak on the grass...

The Marquis immediately retraced his steps, and had no difficulty in finding the cloak. As he turned to leave the lawn again, he saw a brilliant rectangular object at his feet, glittering in the grass at the spot formerly occupied by Monsignor Benedict. He picked it up, in order to return it to its owner–it only required a single glance for him to recognize the roman prelate's velvet-bound steel-boxed missal.

By the time the Marquis got back to the château, everyone else had gone in. While crossing the entrance-hall, he shifted the missal in his hand and the box opened of its own accord between his fingers. He tried to close it again, but could not; it had a secret spring, whose mechanism had doubtless been released when it fell upon the ground.

While Gaston tried to readjust the catch, the pages of the missal opened, and he glanced down at the two exposed pages.

He stopped dead, as if thunderstruck, stifling the cry of amazement that rose unbidden from his breast...

Chapter V
Conversational Trifles

The great hall of the Château de Conflans was arranged for the concert. The orchestra was set on a stage, before which a Nuremberg organ-chest had been placed. Five or six rows of chairs faced the stage, most of them occupied by women and children, in "the costume of the archdiocese," as it was known in the district at the time. These were not ball-gowns–most definitely not; there were chaste sleeveless jackets and decorous wimples everywhere–but nor was it everyday clothing. The dresses were smart and ornaments were worn. The male members of the assembly–priests, aristocrats and civil servants–were standing around the perimeter.

Immediately after entering, Princess de Montfort had sought out Doctor Récamier and laid hold of him, in order to talk to him about the palpitations suffered by her son the Marquis.

"He's a good boy, Doctor," she said, "and so different from his brother, Monsieur le Duc! That one will be the death of me, my nerves are so bad. Whereas Gaston, you know, is exactly the opposite. I don't know why he lost his religious vocation–to me, the boy certainly seems to be cut from clerical cloth. I can't see him in any other garb, and he'd suit a tonsure. The diplomatic corps! I ask you, does he look like a diplomat? But we lost you, Doctor–you weren't with us in the garden. We have been listening to a most original German story-teller, who immediately put us in mind of the Devil... wherever did you get to?"

Her gaze scanned the room and picked out Baron von Altenheimer, who was standing near the entrance door. In the candlelight, the fantastic aspects of his person seemed quite lost. He was probably thirty years of age, but his plainness made him seem older. He had, appropriately enough, one of those faces with which all our readers are familiar, which lasts from the twentieth year until old age and which common parlance calls ageless. He had long, pronounced features, rather pale and drawn, with bushy eyebrows over his sad eyes. His thick hair was brushed down over his forehead, with two thin and lobeless ears projecting from it. His unusually wide mouth wore an expression of naive placidity. His entire physiognomy, in sum, was emphatically bourgeois and common. His carriage was stiffly erect, and his black coat was as distressingly ill-fashioned as his trousers, which were cut several fingerbreadths too short, exposing silk socks of an extreme thinness. His shoes were robust, with pearly buckles.

The Princess noticed that his ankles looked like two knots on a stick.

"There, nevertheless, is the romantic unknown who made us feel an immediate shiver," she continued, laughing. "The moon and darkness are all that is required to play those kinds of tricks! After ten o'clock at night, my niece Madame de Maillé mistakes all the oak-stumps beside the highway for African lions escaped from menageries, and every post for the brigand Rinaldo Rinaldini, about whom she has read in tales of Italy. The gallant German has spoken a great deal about the Danube, but I'm sure that the Danube peasantry has less deplorable tailors. His brother is nice. There's the costume I'd like to see on Gaston!"

Doctor Récamier responded with an assortment of eloquent smiles, as appropriate. Women in general found him extraordinarily attentive. His awesome medical reputation was founded on the most basic of principles: he healed all maladies by prescribing no remedies.

The brother was, indeed, nice–although the word seemed a trifle familiar in the mouth of a princess as a description of a roman prelate in the hall of the Archbishop of Paris. He carried his clerical coat with a proper and perfect grace. His blond hair, smooth and fine, was pierced at the center by a microscopic tonsure; it fell upon his cheeks–which were slightly too rosy–in soft curls, giving him the appearance of a cherub. The Princess was not the cause of that blush; she had used the right word in spite of herself; Monsignor Benedict was nice.

"Hold on!" the Princess went on, touching the Doctor on the arm. "Look over there, at my mirror image!" Her smile, impregnated with that maternal mockery whose falsity always demands contradiction, indicated a tall young man, too slender but very handsome, who was leaning on a window-ledge. His eyes were lowered, perhaps because they had just encountered his mother's.

"Well!" said the Doctor, "I would never have recognized the Marquis de Lorgères. He's grown up into a remarkable cavalier!"

The Princess blushed with pleasure. "Don't you think he's rather too pale?"

"A nervous temperament... an affusion of cold water in a warm bath... a tonic regime without too much excitement... lots of healthy exercise... distraction... I would be honored to pay him a visit..." The Doctor bowed and tactfully withdrew, delicately disengaging his arm from hers.

The Princess fluttered her eyelashes at Gaston, and turned around.

As soon as the Princess had turned her back, Gaston lifted his own eyes again. His gaze, which certainly seemed a trifle feverish, fixed itself on a closed door half-hidden by the orchestra. The Marquis de Lorgères was evidently waiting for someone, and that someone would soon be coming through the door. But was it only anticipation that made his eyes seem hollow and put sweat upon his brow?

At the other end of the room, the Archbishop of Paris approached the Bishop of Hermopolis.

"Is the Baron von Altenheimer a personal acquaintance of yours, My Lord?" he asked.

"Not at all," replied Bishop Frayssinous. "He was presented to me by his brother, who brought me letters of introduction from Cardinals Pacca, Gaysruk and Riario Sforza, as well as a note signed by the prefect of the Congregation of Rites. I know that he has the ear of my colleague at the Ministry of the Interior and of the prefect of police..." He broke off and said: "But here comes the very man! We shall have more information now!"

The prefect of police had indeed come in, and the two prelates could see him exchanging a handshake with Baron von Altenheimer, who was still standing by the door.

"Many of the things he said to us," the Archbishop said, "suggested a mental state which was, to say the least, bizarre..."

"He's a German," Bishop Frayssinous put in, "and a storyteller–two halves of madness!"

"A generous madness–prodigal even," the Archbishop of Paris persisted. "Did you notice that he gave me his pocket-book for Mademoiselle d'Arnheim?"

"I thought I saw that–what was in the pocket-book?"

"A sum so large that I don't know whether it was a mistake on his part. Ten banknotes, a thousand francs each."

"Ten banknotes of a thousand francs!" repeated the astonished Bishop of Hermopolis, before adding, in a lower voice: "But we in France are poor, while these Teutons spend money like water."

The orchestra began playing a motet by Lesueur [19]. Baron von Altenheimer maintained his stiff and awkward posture through the first few bars, but as the French master's majestic and grandiose endeavor was further extended it seemed that the Baron's own stature matured in parallel. His pose altered as he drew himself up to his full height and his breast swelled, filling out the folds of his black coat. Little by little, his eyes lit up for all to see, and his nostrils dilated as if thrust aside by ardent breath. Once again he became the center of attention, instantly acquiring the reputation of an enthusiastic music-lover.

"I fear, your Lordship," the prefect of police replied, in the meantime, to the questions of the Archbishop, "that Wurtemburg has no *chargé d'affaires* in Paris at the moment; Austria is representing its interests for the time being. I will consult the ambassador tomorrow. Messieurs von Altenheimer seem to me to be eminent men and quite dependable. The Baron is a close friend of Prince Metternich–Prince Talleyrand has told me as much... as far as the authenticity of their mission is concerned, it is not my place to comment upon it, alas.

The brothers Ténèbre are evildoers of the most dangerous kind, and we have the dubious honor of their presence in Paris. A bold, extraordinary and highly improbable theft was committed yesterday at the home of His
Lordship the Duc de Bourbon–who is, in fact, one of
Baron von Altenheimer's patrons. Antiques and jewelry
worth more than fifty thousand crowns have been ab-
stracted from his gallery, including three Isabey minia-
tures, five of Madame de Mirbel, two enamels by Petitot
and three rapier-guards that the late prince brought back
from Florence [20]... Her Majesty sent for me today; she
desires to see Baron von Altenheimer."

"And is there any trace of your men?"

"My Lord, Baron von Altenheimer has a brigade of
highly-skilled legal practitioners in his company–including, it is said, two detectives from Scotland Yard...
yes, if you're not familiar with the English police, two
sleuths chosen from the finest that London has to offer...
The King seems to desire that the Baron has a certain
freedom of action... I can only stand aside..."

The prefect of police made no attempt to conceal
his bad humor; he was obviously a little jealous of the
Baron, and thought it outrageous that anyone could dis-
miss his proven troops in favor of the militia of some
petty country no bigger on the map than his thumb.

Whether something happens in the halls of a noble
house or on the footpath of a muddy street, rumor
spreads with a magical rapidity. Within five minutes, the
occupants of the best seats and the remotest recesses
were equally acquainted with the circumstances of the
audacious theft committed by the brothers Ténèbre. No
one had the least doubt that it was the work of the brothers Ténèbre.

The awful celebrity of the brothers Ténèbre, however well its groundwork had been laid by the German's story, had been no more than a light hidden beneath a bushel while the self-interest of the crowd had not been involved. There is a world of difference between a scourge that is only in the mind and a scourge that is alive, menacing and present. Do you remember the immense shock that ran through the social scale from one end of the Seine to the other, in consequence of the sudden fame of that other demon, cholera? Baron von Altenheimer had certainly said that "The brothers Ténèbre are in Paris," but words are worth far less than facts and a fire does not bring forth cries of terror when all one can see is smoke. The brothers Ténèbre had confirmed their presence by what the prefect of police himself had called a "highly improbable" theft. What timing! The German baron went up sharply in everyone's estimation. An immediate link was established between him and the superb bandits, whose Homer he had become. Henceforth, many of the ladies would find something interesting–and strange–in that pale and elongated face, unfortunately attached to those ungraceful shoulders.

The interest was soon further extended. While a circle formed around the two prelates chatting to the prefect of police, a servant came in and handed a letter to the Baron. The servant's livery was unfamiliar. The Baron discreetly acquainted himself with the contents of the letter, shaking his head in a concerned manner and exchanging a few words with his brother; then he crossed the room, his steps determined and ponderous, to stand before the Archbishop of Paris.

"Your Grace," he said, "I had no need, in order to desire an introduction to Your Eminence, of any other motive than the admiration that I have expressed for your person–nevertheless, I did have another motive. I knew that the brothers Ténèbre would come to your episcopal château this evening."

There was a profound silence around the Archbishop, who paled visibly.

"They won't find the Condé gallery here," he murmured, with a smile [21].

"They will find someone that it is in their interest to approach," replied the Baron, "and they know, moreover, that His Lordship the Bishop of Hermopolis will deliver a sermon and raise a collection on behalf of the Christians of the Holy Land."

"That could be postponed," said Bishop Frayssinous.

"I humbly beseech Your Excellencies to do no such thing!" von Altenheimer exclaimed. "To begin with, I give you my word of honor that neither the illustrious master of this house, nor his guests, have anything at all to fear. I have my men all around the château, and twenty-five gendarmes from the Bercy precinct are awaiting His Grace's permission to enter its grounds..."

"It's news to me!" cried the prefect of police.

"They are operating according to the written orders of the Ministry of the Interior," said the Baron, half-withdrawing a large ministerial document from the side pocket of his jacket.

The prefect interrupted the gesture and said, not without a certain resentment: "That's fine... so much the better! They can do without me, for now."

"Illustrious colleague," von Altenheimer replied in a sincere voice, extending both hands towards him, "if I may employ that term with respect to a man such as you, we are joined in a desperate battle here, and I beg you not to withdraw your aid. If the brothers Ténèbre slip through our hands now, they will lose themselves in that Black Forest called London, and the pursuit will have to be handed over to another authority. Have I committed some offence against etiquette or neglected some formality of rank? Forgive me, dear sir–I am a foreigner; my King has charged me with a very difficult task; I am doing my best..."

The honest privy councilor's voice was almost tearful. The two prelates thought that it was their duty to address a few conciliatory words to the prefect. The audience, deeply moved by the idea of the drama that might well reach its climax before their very eyes, and beset by diverse sensations mingling fear, curiosity, expectation, whispered its opinions. That good and noble congregation discovered that it had been conscripted in its entirety–unknowingly, but not against its wishes–to serve as the bait in a rat-trap. That function has a name in the language of thieves which has also lent its color to the speech of honest men: a vile and detestable name which we need not write down because everyone knows it. But what pleasure children take in playing the brigand beneath the great chestnut-trees of the Tuileries!

We all have a little of the child ingrained in us: witness the success, in recent years, of the revival of the innocent pleasures of farcical comedy. We know that everyone loves to dress up and that everyone loves to see others dressed up, the donkey always in the lion's skin and the lion sometimes in the donkey's skin... and then, there is the joy of becoming something else for a little while: the joy of quitting, if only for a moment, the abhorrent role of mere spectator! Think on it! There have been conspiracies–serious and terrible conspiracies–which have no other origin. We can credit to the same account that pure gladness which takes possession of the human being at the thought of a prank, and which grows in direct proportion to the social standing of those who plan the escapade. Does a king not derive a thousand times as much pleasure from playing truant than a schoolboy?

It would not be overly reckless to declare that everyone at the château of His Lordship the Archbishop of Paris that evening was something of a policeman–everyone, that is, with the exception of the prefect of police, who was thinking of handing in his resignation. Dukes and princesses, lovely wives and charming daughters, ordained priests, peers of the realm and cross-bred sons alike surprised themselves by throwing themselves wholeheartedly into a game of cops and robbers. The concert had a new twist, courtesy of a different kind of music. What disguise would the two bold villains have adopted to gain entry to the home of the Archbishop? Through what keyhole had they come? There were imaginative marquises who could already see the Chevalier Ténèbre in a cardinal and brother Ange the vampire in a young German canoness...

Baron von Altenheimer was certainly a clever man, for he sensed the common sentiment and immediately exploited it. "Illustrious people," he said, as if he were addressing a prayer to the whole gathering, "I can say that my fate is in our hands. I have let you in on my secret without being forced to do so. Join with me in an endeavor which is both important and noble, given that our victory could save the fortunes of many families and the lives of a great many Christians. Be on your guard! I can guarantee that the brothers Ténèbre will be here within the hour. Take account, therefore, of any unfamiliar face among those of your friends and acquaintances. Remember that the range of their disguises is limited by the nature of their physiques: one tall, one short, rather like the figurative relationship that exists between my beloved brother and myself. They could present themselves as an old man and a young one, a husband and his wife, or a father and his daughter..."

As he pronounced these last words, the sliding doors behind the orchestra opened. A young woman dressed in white, escorted by an old man of considerable stature, appeared on the stage.

The sight of them caused a shiver to run through the assembled audience...

Chapter VI
O Fount of Love!

The young woman was Mademoiselle d'Arnheim, the Archbishop's *protégée*, who had no wish to earn forty thousand francs in the theatre; the old man was her father. If the Princess had glanced at that moment towards the window-bay in which her son Gaston was standing she would certainly have been astonished by the change wrought in his features.

Gaston de Lorgères was, as we have said, a handsome young man, of an excessively timid and slightly faint appearance. His mother, who loved him madly, nevertheless entertained some doubts as to the scope of his intelligence. She still saw him as a child, and wondered why the spark of virility had not sprung forth within the peaceful adolescence which seemed to have lasted far beyond his twentieth year.

Many a noble husband, it is said, does not know the first thing about the heart of his wife; one might add that many a noble mother struggles in vain to fathom the mind of her son, even though the book lies open before her eyes. Noble mothers often have not the least gift for intellectual rapport; a working-class mother knows her Charles or Jean-Marie, but Madame la Duchesse is often totally ignorant of Monsieur le Comte or Monsieur le Marquis.

What would have astonished the Princess de Montfort, at that moment, was that the spark in question was springing forth in a newly-conceived passion. He was still pale and his large black eyes had lost none of their timidity, but beneath his half-closed eyelids there was a gleam of brightness. He was a statue of flesh and bone, for the moment, but there was a soul within that marble. I doubt that even the affusions of cold water in a warm bath prescribed by Doctor Récamier could have calmed the beating of that heart. Although it is impossible to put the judgement to the test, I fear that palpitations of that sort require a different kind of remedy.

The flame that burned between Gaston's long eyelashes was directed towards a particular target. His gaze was riveted to the young girl in the white dress who had stepped forward on to the stage. The Archbishop of Paris had said, in speaking of her, "my angelic *protégée*." He had not exaggerated. The wonderful oval of her face, framed by shining blonde hair, did indeed resemble the delicate profiles which the imagination of great art has lent to celestial envoys. She seemed to be about eighteen years old at the very most. It was as if her clear and soft expression were veiled by melancholy. She was as beautiful as a dream of Raphael...

Now then! Fantasy has its limits, has it not? Could it really be the case that this seemingly seraphic head belonged to brother Ange Ténèbre, the vampire? We raise the issue because that thought had taken feverish possession of three-quarters of the assembly. Everyone had measured with a single glance the proportional relationship of the Baron von Altenheimer and his young brother, Monsignor Benedict. It was certainly very close to that pertaining to the adorable young girl and the old man who accompanied her. The last words of the Baron, listing the possible disguises of the brothers Ténèbre, had been a father and his daughter and here, coming on the scene as if on cue, were a young girl and her father!

You must take due note of the fact that the brothers Ténèbre were capable of anything. Had not the vampire played the role of the Spanish *Infanta* in Stuttgart? Fifty gazes avidly interrogated Baron von Altenheimer, who had taken up his position beside the entrance door once again, and Monsignor Benedict, who was standing beside him–but the Baron remained impassive, and Monsignor Benedict maintained a honeyed smile upon his lips. Bear in mind, if you will, that this proved nothing: they were two artful men, and it was necessary that the brothers Ténèbre had no clue that their presence was suspected.

She was certainly beautiful, that young girl, but there were many among the assembled women who found, on due consideration, something intimidating about her. What was it? What caused those vague feelings of unease? It was neither the clear blue of her eyes, nor the delicate tint of her complexion, nor the virginal purity of her bearing, nor the halo of her blonde hair. No–it was nothing in particular, but rather the whole ensemble. That was it! She was simply too beautiful!

As regards the old man, the Chevalier Ténèbre had hidden his satanic brow well beneath that venerable mass of snowy hair. That hadn't happened overnight. What deep wrinkles! What a ravaged complexion! What strength of character! But what mortal sadness! One could go to the Great Hungarian Plain and search beneath the crop-fields for the black graves; one could lift up the stones which carried the mysterious inscriptions. There would be nothing there! One would have to look elsewhere for the Chevalier Ténèbre and the vampire priest.

The orchestra played two long chords, followed by a battery of arpeggios, to which accompaniment Mademoiselle d'Arnheim sang Haydn's *Fons Amoris*. She had a *mezzo-soprano* voice of magnificent integrity and incomparable worth. The women had expected a *contralto*, but they were no longer held back by the objections of rationality. What use is reason when it runs up against things that are irrational, mad, impossible, supernatural? In any other circumstances, they would have admired, perhaps passionately, the almost pious manner–expressive of asceticism, of divine candor even–in which Mademoiselle d'Arnheim interpreted the work of the Viennese master. They were connoisseurs; the tender majesty of style could not have escaped them, not the splendor of the voice–but, I ask you, what did all that signify when it was a matter of diabolical illusion? Were they even listening? I don't know. If they were listening to anything, it was the insistent and confused poetry of their fevered brains...

In his window-bay, Gaston drank deliriously from that enchanted cup; by the door, Monsignor Benedict put his open hand over his eyes, doubtless to hide his inquisitive expression. The latter was playing the dilettante, but the Princess, who was on the lookout, thought she saw a piercing gleam between the fingers. It was the Monsignor's eyes, fixed upon Mademoiselle d'Arnheim.

When the last note died within the throat of the *virtuosa*, and while the orchestra played its final chords, Baron von Altenheimer–who had remained until now as stiff as a bronze statue–gave a noisy lead to the applause. The women immediately followed his lead, thinking that they were playing their part. The two prelates–and, for

the most part, the male half of the assembly–were entirely sincere in their long-drawn-out applause. It was a
veritable triumph; the unanimity of the acclamation was
broken by a single protestation. Gaston alone did not
applaud, because his two hands were tightly clasped
upon his heart.

It was not the custom in His Grace's salons to be-
stow noisy ovations upon the artistes, but everyone con-
curred in this instance in prolonging the tribute; feigned
enthusiasm came to the aid of genuine enthusiasm, and
one would have to look to the pits of theaters to obtain
some idea of the din which lasted for several minutes in
the Archbishop's hall.

There was one singular circumstance. At the first
bravos, the tall figure of the old man, who had taken a
seat to the left of the orchestra and slightly of the rear,
came erect again. Painful surprise could be read in his
eyes, like an expression of wounded pride; then his
white head fell upon his breast again, and two large tears
ran down his cheeks.

Mademoiselle d'Arnheim, blushing from her shoulders to her forehead, bowed deeply, took hold of her father's arms, and disappeared.

Archbishop de Quélen made a tour of the room,
collecting opinions with paternal pleasure. Everywhere
one heard the same things. How charming! Perfectly
charming! An admirable voice! What spirit! Marvelous
style! Those whose ears had played them false or rendered them deaf–the majority of those in the concert-
hall–spoke more loudly than the sensitive, and those
women who were putting their hearts and souls into their
new profession made the warmest bids of all.

Baron von Altenheimer had become a statue once
more. His expression, as mysterious as a closed book,

made no response whatsoever to all the beautiful eyes that were fixed upon it. The moment had not yet arrived; it was necessary to be prudent.

There was, however, one curiosity that was closer to the boil and stronger than all the other impatiences. The Princess could not take it any longer. She turned towards her son, who was dreaming–God only knows of what–in his window-bay, and she beckoned to him urgently.

The Marquis de Lorgères roused himself, and obeyed.

"Gaston," the Princess said to him in a low and very mysterious voice, "do you understand what is happening here?"

"What is happening, Madame?" Gaston replied. "Yes, of course."

"Would you do me a favor?"

"With pleasure."

"Go strike up a conversation... discreetly, you understand... with Baron von Altenheimer, and..." She interrupted herself, somewhat discouraged. "But you're so timid, my poor boy." Then she added, presumably to herself: "And so simple!"

"What?" Gaston demanded, in a manner that his mother thought distinctly unappreciative.

"And ask him to tell you, in confidence," she went on, with a smile of renewed hopefulness, "whether those were they for whom we are looking out."

"They?" Gaston repeated. "Which they do you mean, Madame, if you please?"

The Princess tapped her foot and replied: "In God's name! The brothers Ténèbre!"

Gaston stared at her, utterly stupefied. The Princess saw immediately that hope had misled her. Gaston's hauteur had evaporated. "Go," she said, regardless, "and do what you can."

Gaston did not hesitate. He went immediately to-wards Baron von Altenheimer. His mother followed him with her eyes and said to herself: "His brother, the Duc, has matured perfectly well. Poor Gaston is obviously retarded. One must accept whatever one gets."

At that moment, Gaston resolutely set himself be-side the Baron, who greeted him with the same fulsome gestures that he extended to everyone. Gaston did not seem disconcerted. A conversation was quickly estab-lished between himself and Baron von Altenheimer. Gaston spoke, in truth, very freely and made himself heard.

How happy his mother was! Doubly delighted–for she was witness to the progress of her son and her son was the bearer of her news–the happy mother triumphed in her heart and in her mind. Whatever one gets; the dictum of all mothers!

This, however, was how Gaston, Marquis of Lor-gères, accomplished the highly confidential mission en-trusted to him by the Princess.

"Monsieur le Baron," he said, "I have listened to you this evening with a good deal of pleasure and inter-est."

"I am grateful to Monsieur le Marquis..." the Ger-man began.

"And you will understand better," Gaston contin-ued, "when you know that the remarkable subject of your tale is conjoined, for me, with a series of family considerations. We are, Monsieur le Baron, first cousins once removed of Field-Marshal Victor de Rohan, Prince de Guémenée, Duc de Rohan, de Bouillon and de Mon-bazon, who actually resides in Hungary..."

Von Altenheimer bowed.

"And as the heads of the family of the late duchess," the young Marquis continued, "who died childless, as you must know, we possess several properties there, near Debrecen, which are not let but are quite considerable..."

The Princess, meanwhile, was saying to herself: "What's this? What's he saying now? Monsieur le Baron seems to be paying very close attention to him!"

This was nothing less than the truth: Baron von Altenheimer was all ears. Gaston continued: "After certain digressions which added much, from my point of view, to the piquancy of your tale, I saw that you were pleased to conceal beneath the frivolous spirit of the storyteller a considerable depth of actual knowledge..."

"Ah, Monsieur de Marquis..."

"If you will permit me... This is not a compliment, but a matter of preparing the way to ask you a great favor."

"I am entirely at your disposal," the Baron said.

"A thousand thanks... it concerns our properties in Hungary... my brother, the Duc, was the victim of a certain youthful recklessness, and when he came into a part of his inheritance, he was able to mortgage the estate of Niszar. It is seven hundred leagues from Paris to Debrecen. Without making any accusation against German or Hungarian lawyers, I merely state the facts: the Niszar estate has been sold at public auction to pay the mortgagees..."

"How long ago was this?" the Baron asked, sharply.

"Three years ago, perhaps four..."

"You are sure that five years have not passed?"

"Perfectly sure. My brother, Monsieur le Duc, was only seventeen then."

"And he must have had time to squander the estate. That's right... I'm with you, Monsieur le Marquis."

"I have heard some report," Gaston continued, earnestly, "of the Hungarian laws regulating the right of repurchase after a forced sale, but no Magyar authors have been translated into French and their use of Latin idiom does not always seem clear to me... Mayruth fixed at four years the period of facultative redemption and the full right..."

"Mayreuth," said the Baron, correcting the spelling of the name, "is an obstinate pedant who is no longer read... the Austrian court, in giving Hungary the benefit of its ancient legislation, has codified the matter. The legal period of redemption and the automatic right of repurchase is five years and a day from the date of the public auction... and it is not without precedent for the period to be extended on the basis of a request submitted to the Chancellery, with supporting documents..."

Gaston bowed ceremoniously in his turn.

"Monsieur le Baron," he said, taking his leave, "I beg you to accept all my thanks."

"Now then, Marquis," his mother said to herself as he came back towards her, "do me the favor of giving me the three essential points of that sermon you preached to him?"

"Madame," Gaston replied, with a smile that the Princess had never seen before, "I have begun my diplomatic career. These privy councilors, it seems to me, are very difficult to get around."

"He did not want to answer your question?"

"Indeed he did."

"Tell me, then," the Princess said, petulantly. "Tell me immediately."

"Mother, Monsieur le Baron told me that the two men in question are here..."

"Oh! I was sure of it!"

"But no one," the young Marquis finished, calmly, "has recognized them: neither you, nor anyone here, has identified them as yet."

"Oh!" repeated the Princess, in a very different manner. "He's just making fun of you."

Gaston kissed her hand with a grace that made her think again. "Madame," he replied, with a slight hint of mockery that completed her discomfiture, "would you like me to do you a second and even better favor?"

"What, Gaston?"

"Would you like me to go into the next room, to talk to Monsieur d'Arnheim himself?"

"And ask him if he is the Chevalier Ténèbre?" The Princess laughed.

"To find out without asking him, Madame," Gaston corrected.

The Princess took him by the hand and put her mouth very close to his ear. "If you can do that, Gaston," she said, "I will give you a Tilbury carriage like the one your brother has."

"I would prefer something else, Madame," the young Marquis replied, gravely.

"What then? Tell me."

"Only promise," Gaston replied, "not to talk about me to my cousin Emerance for six weeks."

The Princess burst out laughing, showing her teeth–which were still quite beautiful.

"Monsieur le Marquis," she said, "I forbid you to fall in love! Someone must have waved a magic wand over you." She pointed a finger at him tenderly and added: "Go! And find out whether this Mademoiselle d'Arnheim is really an old priest dead for four hundred years!"

The young Marquis negotiated a passage towards Archbishop de Quélen and said to him: "My Lord, my mother has asked me to speak to Monsieur d'Arnheim about the possibility of taking lessons."

"Excellent!" murmured the Archbishop, who took Gaston by the hand, led him to the door situated behind the orchestra, and opened it. "My good Monsieur d'Arnheim," he said, raising his voice, "I bring you an ambassador. This is the beginning. If it pleases God, our dear child will soon be obliged to refuse lessons!" He closed the door behind Gaston.

There was no one in the room but the old man and the girl. Mademoiselle d'Arnheim, at the sight of the young Marquis, changed color two or three times. Her father lowered his eyes while the vivid blush showed on her cheeks.

Gaston, so eloquent a moment ago, stood before them with a pale face and silent lips.

Chapter VII
A Proposal of Marriage

On the other side of the door the concert continued. The Nuremberg organ warbled beneath the fingers of Monsignor Benedict, who was playing a charming ditty, the famous Bolognese Christmas carol *Jesu Bambino*.

As for our three individuals, the silence had not yet been broken and the unease was growing. Monsieur d'Arnheim finally made an effort to overcome the awkwardness, and began: "You came, Monsieur, to discuss with me the possibility of lessons to be given by my daughter...?"

He stopped. No words are adequate to describe the humiliated pride, the crushed nobility, the bitter regret, mingled with resignation, melancholy and love, with which the old man pronounced those few words.

Gaston took a step towards him.

"Prince," he said, in a low voice, "you are mistaken. That is not why I am here."

"Prince!" echoed Monsieur d'Arnheim, whose limbs had begun to tremble, while his daughter hid her tearful face between her hands. "Prince...!" Then, placing his tremulous wrists on the arms of his chair as he made ready to rise to his feet, he said: "Who do you think you are talking to, Monsieur?"

"I know," Gaston replied, his voice having hardened again, "that I am talking to Chrétien Baszin, Prince Jacobyi."

The old man slumped back in his seat. "Who told you that?" he demanded, darkly.

"Lenore, your daughter."

"Lenore! My daughter!" He turned towards Mademoiselle d'Arnheim, whose hands were clasped together as if in prayer, perhaps to implore Gaston to be quiet.

Monsieur d'Arnheim stood up. "Who are you?" he demanded.

"Gaston de Montfort, Marquis de Lorgères, second son of the Prince de Montfort."

"Ah!" said Monsieur d'Arnheim, his gaze moving back and forth between the young man and the girl. Then he asked one more time: "What do you want from me, Monsieur le Marquis de Lorgères?"

"I want to ask for the hand of your daughter. I love her, and she loves me." This was said in a distinct voice, with head held high and a steady gaze.

Mademoiselle d'Arnheim had closed her eyes and had let herself fall into a chair.

In the next room, the sweet voice of the Monsignor embellished another carol, harvesting at the end of every verse a rich crop of merited applause.

The old man looked once again at his daughter. It was not anger that was in his eyes; it was bleak despair. "You've deceived me!" he murmured.

Mademoiselle d'Arnheim threw herself towards him. He thrust her back, but not rudely, while he added, addressing himself to Gaston: "Monsieur de Marquis, to take the last possession of a ruined man is to steal from the altar!"

"Father!" cried the girl. "Good and noble father! I will never leave you, and I swear to you that I have never done anything deserving of reproach."

"In that case," said the old man, directing a scornful glance at Gaston, "this is a madman, who should go away!"

"Not before I have your answer, Prince," the young Marquis replied. "I have told the truth: I love your daughter; she loves me; and I ask for her hand."

"You have spoken to this man, Lenore?" Monsieur d'Arnheim demanded.

"Never, Father," she replied, in a faint voice.

"How, then, does he dare to boast...?"

"Father," the young girl interrupted, sliding to her knees, "he is not boasting... but if he knows it, his heart must have told him, for we have never exchanged a word."

"There is a mystery here..." began the old man, whose stern face had gone as white as snow.

His daughter interrupted again: "There is nothing, Father," she said, "but my love for you and our destiny. While you were ill, and after having sold everything that you possessed in the world, it fell to me one day to go in search of medicines without having the money to pay for them. I was refused credit. I sat down on the step of the shop, exhausted and discouraged."

"And you begged for alms, child!" cried Monsieur d'Arnheim, his eyes lighting up.

"I would have done, Father, if I had thought of it. But I was utterly lost, and I thought of nothing but coming back to you, and of dying with you. Monsieur le Marquis was passing by; he stopped before me; I did not see him. Mina had followed me; Mina went towards him..."

As the name Mina was spoken, a little black spaniel came out from beneath Monsieur d'Arnheim's armchair, in order to jump on to a chair and from there to the table next to which Gaston was standing. She began to lick Gaston's hand. The old man averted his eyes.

"I remember that in the depths of my distress I prayed fervently to God," Mademoiselle d'Arnheim continued. "I implored him to work a miracle and to send to my father that manna which the celestial birds had carried to those lost in the desert. When Mina returned, Monsieur le Marquis was no longer there, but Mina put her muzzle between my knees, and in the folds of my dress I saw the glitter of a gold piece..."

Monsieur d'Arnheim let out a groan. Mina leapt with one bound to the carpet and went to comfort him; he pushed her aside as gently and as sadly as he had pushed his daughter away.

"We are Baszins!" he murmured. Then he asked, his voice taking on a different tone: "How was the acquaintance renewed?"

"You have been ill for three months," the young woman replied. "That grand and luxurious residence which you are in the habit of admiring is the town house of the Princess de Montfort; I don't know how Mina knew the way. Whenever the gold piece was spent, Mina went out again, and always returned with manna."

"And you knew whence this manna came, did you not?"

"From God, whose help I had implored, Father."

"And you let Mina out! Had you no shame?"

The old man's lip quivered; his eyelids fluttered like those of a woman fighting to hold back tears.

"Father," said Mademoiselle d'Arnheim in a low voice, "I let Mina out because she brought the breath

96

back to your lungs and the blood to your veins...and I had no shame because I already loved the hand of that God who sent us his manna."

"Thank you," murmured Gaston, his eyes moist.

"But what did you expect? What did you expect?" cried the old man, in anguish.

Mademoiselle d'Arnheim lifted her angelic gaze towards the heavens, and replied: "Father, I put my trust in God."

There was a momentary silence. Monsignor Benedict was still chanting his mild Italian devotions. Monsieur d'Arnheim looked Gaston in the face, then he offered his hand.

"Chrétien Baszin, Prince Jacobyi, as you have called him, and as I called him myself in former times, is indebted to you, Monsieur le Marquis," he said, slowly. "He sees that you are a noble and generous young man. Perhaps he would even have been flattered by your quest in happier times–but he cannot ignore the fact that the house of de Montfort is one of the richest in France. Chrétien Baszin could never permit his daughter to enter such a family as that unless the gate were opened wide; he possesses nothing but his pride. If the Princess de Montfort herself came in search of the Princess Jacobyi, then it might indeed be God's wish to contrive the union of two great houses."

"If that is what is required, that is what will be done," Gaston replied, without hesitation. "I give you my word."

But what, you may ask, of that cousin Emerance to whom the Princess had said too much about Gaston? Was not Monsieur le Marquis being much too forward, for a timid young man? We do not know, to tell the truth, whether his mother would have been delighted or desolated by his words. The chick, it seems, had broken his shell with one blow of his beak and come out in his full plumage.

Gaston shook Monsieur d'Arnheim's hand and respectfully kissed the young woman's; it was a sort of conditional betrothal. Then, raising himself up again, he went on in a brisk tone: "Prince, would you recognize, if chance were to bring you face to face with them, the two gypsies who received hospitality at Chandor Castle, on the night when your daughter was kidnapped?"

Mademoiselle d'Arnheim started in surprise, and became as pale as an alabaster statue.

"How do you know...?" the old man stammered.

"There are many things I need to explain to you, Prince," the young Marquis interrupted, "but this is neither the time or the place. I beg you to be content with answering my question."

"I would recognize them," said Monsieur d'Arnheim, through gritted teeth, "ten years from now!"

Gaston cocked an ear. Monsignor Benedict had finished singing.

"Prince," he went on, "you are destined to find yourself, perhaps this very evening, face to face with those who have accomplished your ruination..."

"Rubbish!" cried the old man.

"We have mentioned God more than once in this interview," said Gaston gravely. "He moves in mysterious ways. A person who seems to me to know what he is talking about has predicted that the brothers Ténèbre will put in an appearance, this evening, in the Archbishop's house. When Mademoiselle d'Arnheim goes to perform again, you will doubtless accompany her. Look around, but be sure to hide your legitimate anger and rightful resentment. It is vitally important to you, to your daughter, and also to me, your future son-in-law, that no one except me penetrates your secret. We shall draw apart from one another, but there must be a signal. If you recognize the two evildoers, promise me two things: make this gesture openly, and no other; and abstain absolutely from taking any action." He touched his right hand to his brow, with all five fingers extended.

Monsieur d'Arnheim hesitated for a moment, then he said: "I trust you, young man, and I will do as you ask."

As soon as he had received that promise, the Marquis de Lorgères bowed twice, putting into the smile that he addressed to Lenore everything that he could not express in words. Then he moved rapidly towards the door opposite to that which had admitted him.

He crossed the hallway, descended the staircase, and went out into the gardens. It was not to calm his simmering blood, nor to refresh his bare head, that the Marquis de Lorgères made this nocturnal expedition. He looked around him attentively as he went, and paused from time to time in order to listen.

The night was black, but Paris was not asleep, and the noise of the city could still be heard in the distance. Above that muted din other sounds, closer and more distinct, were discernible: footsteps, whispers, muffled laughs. All around the château, the darkness was populated.

Gaston reached the park and found a wooded place. He pushed his way into the heart of a thicket, looked around once more, listened more carefully, and finished by secreting beneath the thickest foliage an object which he took from his bosom.

Then he retraced his steps to the château and went back into the salon by the main door...

Baron von Altenheimer, who seemed to have appointed himself as a concierge, so faithfully had he stuck to his post, gave a slight start of surprise at Gaston's appearance. It was only momentary; afterwards, his face resumed its placid expression.

"Monsieur le Marquis has not heard my brother Benedict, then?" he said.

"Yes indeed," Gaston replied. "Heard, and applauded."

The Monsignor thanked him, and the Baron added: "I did not see you go out, Marquis."

"A little fresh air," Gaston replied, as he went on into the room. "It's stifling in here."

"Monsieur le Marquis," the Princess said to him, in a tone intended to be most severe, "you have been gone thirty-five minutes, by the hands of the clock. Your conduct is extremely improper." But she added, pointing her finger at him: "I shall give you a penance, if you have not brought me a generous armful of news."

"Has nothing happened here?" Gaston asked.

"I have a stiff neck from looking this way and that," the Princess replied. "The Doctor pretends that it is all a huge practical joke. But these devotees of the profound wisdom know nothing, you know... now, Gaston, we are losing our heads. You are interrogating me and I have been good enough to reply—everything is upside-down!"

Gaston remained silent.

"How pale you are," his mother said, uneasily. "You should have brought some color back with you. You owe me an explanation, Gaston my boy. We have begun our first romance, have we not? Be honest! Poor Emerance! Speak, Gaston, I insist. What have you been doing since you left the room?"

"Madame," replied the young Marquis, forced to make the effort to save his dream, "I do not believe that this is a romance, but it is a strange story nevertheless. Tomorrow, if you will permit, I will submit to your levy: I have the greatest need to talk to you."

There is no word to express the passion for knowledge that mothers have. It would be unjust to give the name "curiosity" to such a profound desire. The Princess's astonishment was magnified. She no longer recognized in her son the child of old of whom she had said: "When will the man awaken in him?" The man had awakened, with a definite start! The Princess, completely overtaken, was still searching for the child and no longer understood.

Gaston would not have got away so lightly if there had not been a great stir in the salon. The Bishop of Hermopolis moved towards the stage, and an emotion that had no direct relationship to the sermon that he intended to give took hold of the audience. The appearance of the brothers Ténèbre had been anxiously anticipated since the quest for them had begun. The Archbishop's salon was beset by curious maladies, fears, desires and fevers–none of which, most assuredly, had anything to do with the unfortunate Christians of the Holy Land.

As the Bishop of Hermopolis took his position on the stage, the Princess only had time to say: "Will you tell me, at least, who these people are–the d'Arnheims?"

"You shall know tomorrow, Mother," Gaston replied, as he moved away. "It is for precisely that reason that I need to see you."

Bishop Frayssinous began to speak, commanding silence.

There are still many people alive who were personally acquainted with the illustrious author of the *Défense de la Religion.* All of them agree in saying that the public eloquence of the Bishop of Hermopolis was distinguished above all by measured argument, moderation and an abundance of proofs deduced with calm authority and certitude; but they add that his private eloquence was another thing entirely. He had a southern ardor in his blood and a lively impulse to charity in his heart. When he went into battle against the selfishness of worldly men for the purpose of extracting alms, he was not a regular soldier in the apostolic army but a lightly-armed sharpshooter: a *zouave* [22], if such an anachronism is permissible. He never retreated; he was prepared to make arrows from any kind of wood. One recalls what Monsieur de Talleyrand said of the sermon preached at the home of the Duchesse d'Angoulême on behalf of the widows and orphans of the war in Greece: "He had our charity by the throat!"

In this instance, his theme was just as real and even more urgent; it concerned those unhappy Christian families scattered throughout Palestine and groaning under Turkish domination. In more recent times, the Eastern war has educated us on that subject, and no one is ignorant of the lamentable barbarities which formerly cast a shadow on the light of the guiding stars of our century, but there was at that time an almost impassable barrier between Europe and those cries of agony. Their first harrowing echo was, however, heard that evening in the hall of the Château de Conflans.

Bishop Frayssinous had, moreover, to contend with a general inattention, for the fever that had gripped the crowd was a rude rival to his speech. After several minutes had passed, though, that inattention had been tamed, and every face took on an expression of intense concentration, directed towards a common focus: the orator.

102

All those previously-stifled moans; all those previously-unheard cries, all those groans extracted by long and intolerable torture, were reunited in one single voice to burst forth like a thousand simultaneous death-rattles in the bosom of that rich, brilliant and happy assembly. The discourse did not last long, but when it ended there was sweat on every brow and a tear in every eye.

The Bishop of Hermopolis came down from the stage then, and the Archbishop of Paris embraced him effusively before handing him the huge red velvet purse in which the collection was to be taken.

As soon as he took his first step, the prelate began to accumulate an abundant harvest of gold pieces and banknotes. The force of good example mingled with that desire to emulate which peevish philosophers call vanity. The Marsh apparatus extracts arsenic from the same soil that gives us wheat for outer bread [23]; in the moral order, as in the physical order, is there anything on Earth that is entirely pure? Having rendered the eternal negative in answer to that question, the point of great and good works is to ameliorate intoxication, to tame passion, and to direct impetuousness towards a noble end. The Princess donated her bracelet. From that moment on, jewelry rained into the increasingly-heavy and swollen purse. Ear-rings, brooches and strings of pearls hastened to join the Princess's bracelet. Charity also has its auctions.

"Monsieur le Baron," said the Bishop of Hermopolis, as he arrived at the entrance-door, "I know that you have already despoiled yourself on behalf of another unfortunate; I shall take care to ask nothing of you."

Baron von Altenheimer was in the process of making a little paper trumpet out of an envelope. He was doing his best, but his large clumsy hands were making rather a mess of it.

"Give, my dear brother Benedict," he said, after an interval when he paid no attention to His Excellency.

Monsignor Benedict removed from his finger the exceedingly beautiful solitaire which had excited the admiration of the assembly, and dropped it into the purse. It was a gift fit for a king. The Bishop of Hermopolis bowed and was about to pass on, when the Baron said to him: "If you would graciously permit it, Your Lordship, I would like to keep a little snuff—it is a distinctly tyrannical habit..."

The bishop turned back. Into the little trumpet he had fabricated, rather awkwardly, Baron von Altenheimer was busy emptying the contents of his splendid gold snuff-box encrusted with diamonds the size of peas. Having achieved the transfer, he slipped the box into the purse, adding with perfect simplicity: "A thousand thanks, Your Lordship."

The box was worth three or four times as much as the ring. The gesture had a tremendous effect, especially the little trumpet and the thousand thanks. More than one person wondered whether the kingdom of Wurtemburg, which had the honor of harboring the Black Forest within its narrow bounds, might actually be Eldorado.

The brothers von Altenheimer had resumed their peaceful and modest attitudes, and the Bishop of Hermopolis continued his collection, which had already produced a fortune.

"Mademoiselle d'Arnheim, for the finale," said Archbishop de Quélen, signaling to the orchestra. One of the musicians went in search of the *virtuosa*.

Gaston had his offering in his hand at the moment when Monsieur d'Arnheim and his daughter reappeared on the stage. He saw the avid gaze of the old man make a rapid tour of the room and come to a halt, staring fixedly at the entrance-door, next to which the two brothers Altenheimer were standing in isolation.

The reaction experienced by Monsieur d'Arnheim was so violent that he staggered like a man about to fall backwards.

"Well, Marquis," said the Bishop, whose purse had been extended towards Gaston for several seconds.

"Well, Gaston," repeated the Princess, who was watching him. "He has given silver," she gasped, almost immediately afterwards, as she collapsed into an arm-chair. "Doctor, he has given silver! My son, to the collection of the Minister of Ecclesiastical Affairs! For the Christians of the Holy Land! Mademoiselle d'Arnheim must indeed be an ancient ecclesiastic! See! Gaston is mad! That's an enchantress in flesh and bone! He's twenty-three years old! Are there affusions of cold water administered in warm baths powerful enough to prevent young men from behaving like idiots? I have longed for him to assert himself a little, but not like this! Lord Above! The Duc has already tried to drive me mad. And can you imagine, to cap it all, that he does not want to hear talk of his cousin Emerance–a charming girl, in good standing at court?"

She aired her grievances as best she could, but we must admit to you, in confidence, that there was a smile beneath her anger.

The Bishop also laughed as he left the young Marquis, whose hand had let three forty-*sou* pieces fall into his collection: the only ones! He realized well enough that a mistake had been made.

But Gaston was not laughing; his entire being was in his eyes. I do not know whether he had even noticed the look of timid tenderness that Mademoiselle d'Arnheim had darted towards him while entering. He had eyes for no one but her father: her father, whose white hair quivered on his forehead.

Slowly, so very slowly, Monsieur d'Arnheim lifted his right hand to his forehead, on which the five trembling fingers rested for a moment, fully outstretched.

Gaston let out a deep sigh, and lost himself in the crowd.

Chapter VIII
The End of the Soirée

The brothers Ténèbre had not yet put in an appearance. The two prelates, the prefect of police and a few other important people were counting up the collection in a small room just off the hall, whose door stood open, while Mademoiselle d'Arnheim sang Mozart's *Ave Verum*, accompanied by the orchestra.

The admirable artiste surpassed herself in rendering the admirable work. The quiet crowd was all ears, when everyone was suddenly subjected to a violent shock. Baron von Altenheimer half-opened the entrance-door and shouted at the top of his voice: "Look out!"

At the same time, he threw himself into the neighboring room where their Lordships were.

From the other side of the half-open main door, several voices replied: "Yes!"

The Monsignor was already at a window, rapidly turning the handle that would release its lock. "Look out, everyone!" he cried, cupping his hands like a megaphone.

From all sides, distant voices replied from the park: "Yes! Yes! Yes!"

There is no need to add that the orchestra and the singer immediately fell silent.

There was a moment of indescribable tumult. The first woman's scream gave birth to a hundred, as is always the case. The men in the great hall launched themselves towards the small room, those in the little room raced back into the larger one.

Not one of them saw anything, search as he might, but everyone believed that others had seen something. By the time three minutes had gone by, two dozen women had fainted.

"Here! In the garden!" cried a voice from outside.

There was a sudden surge towards the window.

"Here, on the stairs!" shouted another voice.

The door was shut.

Gunshots were heard in the distance.

Baron von Altenheimer reappeared then, with his big black coat buttoned up. His head was held high and his eyes shone.

"I must beg your pardon," he said, calmly. "Come, brother Benedict... I will have them, or die trying!"

The Monsignor also had the bearing of a little hero. They hurled themselves through the door together and disappeared, amid the myriad pleas of women begging them not to expose themselves to any risk.

Once they had made their exit, the hue and cry faded into the distance, then died away.

When three more minutes had passed, a profound silence reigned in the hall of the Château de Conflans. No one said a word, save for two men half-hidden behind the orchestra, one of whom was struggling as hard as he could against the other.

"Why did you stop me?" Monsieur d'Arnheim demanded, exhausted by his efforts.

"Prince," replied Gaston, Marquis de Lorgères, "I give you my word of honor that they shall not escape!"

Others were coming out of their trance. Each one took hold of himself and looked at his neighbors. So little trace of the tempest remained all around them that it might all have been a dream. Besides, the von Altenheimers were gone. Everyone listened; no one felt obliged to speak. Everyone felt a vague apprehension growing in himself: an uneasy impression of having been duped.

There was no longer any noise of footsteps outside, nor of shouting, not of gunshots.

The Archbishop was the first to speak. "There is something inexplicable in this business."

"These conflicts of interest between the Minister of the Interior and the Prefecture are an outrage!" the prefect of police added, peevishly.

"Did you see something, Madame la Marquise?" the Princess asked her neighbor.

"Something, Madame? No, I cannot tell you what I have seen. I closed my eyes, as one does when gunshots ring out in the theatre... but I sensed... oh, I am sure that I smelled something burning..."

"Aunt," cried Madame de Maillé. "Leonie saw a man in black."

"I saw it too," said the doctor. "A huge hairy body..."

There was some laughter. Perhaps it only required a frank and well-chosen word to turn the whole thing into a joke, but the word was not forthcoming.

The Bishop of Hermopolis said: "Let's finish counting the collection." But he had hardly put a foot into the little room when he made an exclamation of amazement.

The jumpy nerves of the audience had settled a little; there was no renewal of the panic. But as His Excellency, rather than stepping back, hurled himself towards the table which occupied the center of the little room, he was followed across the threshold by several other men and a few women.

His Excellency, who stood before the table with his head lowered and all strength gone from his arms, was soon surrounded.

"Mercy!" cried Archbishop de Quélen, wringing his hands. "Our collection!" That was all that was said. The noble assembly fell into that particular species of silence which follows utter mystification.

The table was bare. Not one of the objects lately contained by the red velvet purse was to be seen.

"See!" said the prefect of police, eventually. "If the Minister of the Interior had only consulted my people..."

"Monsieur!" interrupted the Archbishop, with a wrath whose wellspring was the frustration of his charity. "There was not only the Ministry of the Interior in this, but the Court of Rome and the Chancellery of the Kingdom of Wurtemburg! We have lost the wealth of the poor, and someone is making a mockery of us!"

"One tall, and one short," murmured the Princess, repeating the words that Baron von Altenheimer had spoken for the first time in the verdant arena.

"It was them! It was them!" twenty voices cried at the same time.

"The Baron is the Chevalier Ténèbre..."

"And the Monsignor is brother Ange, the vampire!"

Chapter IX
An Essay on the Philosophy of Theft

All men whose trade is deception, or the foiling of deception–which is to say, all game and all hunters; for
example, the admirable thieves of London, who learn
their profession at a university, and the equally admirable detectives of Scotland Yard who are trained to follow their tracks across the pavements of that great
Babylon–will tell you that there are two principal methods of rendering oneself invisible, not including Alad-
din's lamp. One is to hide, the other to display oneself
while covering one's face with a mask; to lurk in the
shades of night, or to confront the light of the sun val-
iantly.

In two words: cunning and audacity.

Cunning is primarily associated with the old school;
audacity is the *forté* of the modern movement. The majority of the gentlemen savants whose field of study is
the art of thievery recommend audacity very highly, and
do not scruple to say that wiliness has had its day. The
honorable Josuah J. Marshall [24], the pride of the London
criminal fraternity, who was sentenced to hang at the
Old Bailey as the reign of King George neared its end,
put it thus: "Tell the constable that you are Jack Sheppard and he will not believe you; prove to him, by means
of your birth-certificate, that you are Jack Sheppard;

steal his watch, his purse, his shirt and his truncheon, and he will laugh, saying: Get away! Jack Sheppard!"

In all good things, you can be certain, the spirit of the English will find the extreme; but there is a great deal of truth in the opinion of the honorable Josuah J. Marshall, and the fact that he was hanged does not disprove his theory. A true gentleman of the criminal fraternity accepts the inevitability of the noose philosophically, as the rest of us are forced to accept the inevitability of death. It is, in either case, a mere matter of time; that is a fact of life. The issue at hand is to live as well as one can, or to put off being hanged as long as possible. Josuah J. Marshall attained the ripe old age of eighty-three years before being hanged. He bequeathed his methods and his philosophy to his children and his children's children.

Now go into the prisons and ask the governors by what means their boarders most frequently escape. Their response will be unanimous: however they can. Do not be content with that overly vague reply; get to the bottom of the question. Establish the categories. It will not put the jailer in a good mood, of that you can be sure, because you will put your finger on some remembered wound, ancient or modern, but in the end you will know this: there are more escapes at noon than midnight, more by the main gate than by underground tunnels. The majority escape with heads held high, faces bare and a smile upon their lips, bowing politely to the concierge's wife and saying "Good-day, my friend" to the guard.

The human mind is made that way; it has a passion for contradiction. Precautions can, in the final analysis, only be excited or intensified by the affirmation: "I am not a thief." That is sufficient in itself to provide a constable or a gendarme with a motive to put you to the test in case you are a liar. But say to him "I am a thief" and he will feel a perfectly natural temptation to try and prove the opposite.

This is a serious matter. There was recently to be found in London, behind Drury Lane, a very respectable place where practitioners of the art demonstrated various ways of picking a lock without spoiling it. The course was open to the public, and we had the honor of being present–Rule Britannia! Whereas the preceding considerations were matters of university education, this was a primary school.

If Baron von Altenheimer and Monsignor Benedict really had been the brothers Ténèbre, they had obviously employed the Marshall procedure. Except that, as the German bandits were still studying their Plutarch, they had been obliged to build up their own reputation in the Archbishop's salon and sing their own epic. Then they had cried out, after the fashion of the honorable Josuah J. Marshall: "We are the brothers Ténèbre!"

And no one had believed them.

They had, to be sure, not said it in so many words, but they had arranged matters in such a way that the thought had occurred to everyone–and that thought had, indeed, occurred to everyone at the given moment; but everyone had said, like the constable to Josuah J. Marshall: "The brothers Ténèbre! Get away!"

Once a thought has come to knock at the door of the imagination, and has been refused its hospitality, everything is set: the blindfold is covering your eyes, tied in a triple knot. That is the real import of the calculation.

Now, gentlemen of the second rank have been seen to operate in this jolly manner by taking the name of Jack Sheppard. Had the von Altenheimers, then, stolen the identities of the brothers Ténèbre? Where did the

113

falsehood end within their tale? Did the brothers Ténèbre actually exist, or was there not even an atom of truth at the bottom of their shameless lies?

The prefect of police climbed into the first available carriage and returned to Paris at full speed. The ability of that eminent magistrate is proverbial; undoubtedly, he must have put the battalions of his secret army into the field without delay. He found not the least trace, however, in the archives of the Prefecture, of the Chevalier Ténèbre or of brother Ange the vampire, nor the least trace of Baron von Altenheimer or Monsignor Benedict. It appeared that mounting a hunt for an oupire and a vampire was no trivial enterprise!

The remainder of His Lordship's guests withdrew sadly. The good Archbishop, on going to his room, kept one secret consolation in the depths of his heart. There remained to him, to lighten the burden of his misfortune very slightly, the certainty that the pocket-book destined for Mademoiselle d'Arnheim had never left his person. He wanted to count the banknotes again.

Alas, the pocket-book had vanished, along with His Lordship's magnificent pastoral cross!

Chapter X
The Missal

That evening the Princess de Montfort did not have the hand of her usual cavalier to help her down from her carriage. For the first time, the Marquis had left his mother in the lurch.

The Princess was a strong-minded woman, as we have observed, and the opinion of all strong minds is that the doors should be thrown wide open once youth has reached its end. But among women, especially strong-minded women, there is a world of difference between theory and practice. One paltry ghost story had brought the Princess's entire body out in gooseflesh, even though she did not believe in ghosts. Youth must come to an end, but the Princess was decidedly heartsick when she took the hand of Doctor Récamier as she mounted the steps of her townhouse.

"You have a touch of fever, my lady," the Doctor said to her, "and I'm not surprised, after everything that has happened. Take my advice: have a nice warm bath tomorrow morning, with a simple affusion of cold water."

"When I think, Doctor," the Princess sighed, "that I took that *demoiselle* d'Arnheim for... oh, the shameless villains! Leonie felt a hairy hand... she's a little mad, poor thing... but look at Gaston, with the bit between his teeth! Oh, I hope he's done the right thing, leaving the seminary! She's pretty, at least. There's nothing to be said. And poor Emerance has a slight squint... but not unbecoming, eh? What a party! It was too terrible, Doctor!"

The Doctor took his leave, saying: "In a nice warm bath, my lady, a simple affusion."

If anyone had asked the Princess where her son was at that moment, she would have replied without hesitation and with perfect confidence: "My son Gaston is prowling around Mademoiselle d'Arnheim." She might perhaps have added, in her capacity as a strong-minded woman: "At least the Duc never chases after angels!"

In spite of her long experience and ample powers of deduction, the Princess would have been in error in this case. Gaston was not prowling around Mademoiselle d'Arnheim; Gaston was all alone, making his way on foot across the three leagues that separated the Château de Conflans from the Rue de l'Université.

Gaston had indeed escorted Monsieur d'Arnheim and his daughter as far as the humble carriage that awaited them at the gate of the château, but there he had left them, saying to the old man: "Whatever time it may be when I call on you tonight, you must see me; you will understand the reasons for my actions then." He had then gone back towards the château, but instead of going in to find his mother, who would have pestered him for news, he had circled the building and then gone back into the park.

The moon was hidden; the sky was still full of huge, heavy and slow-moving clouds, through which its light occasionally showed for brief intervals. Gaston retraced the route that he had followed during the soirée; he seemed very agitated. When he reached the patch of woodland the darkness was so deep that he hesitated, unsure of his path.

The mysterious noises that he had heard earlier within the park and its environs had ceased now. All was silent save for the distant murmur of the great city, whose presence also revealed itself by the red tint reflected from the low clouds that lay over it.

Such fears are childish! thought the Marquis de Lorgères. Even so, I have heard it said that the whole world is vulnerable to such effects, including the King... I am no exception.

He had passed into an elmwood, whose undergrowth was composed of thorn-bushes and privet, entwined with serpentine honeysuckle. It was here that he had come during the soirée; he remembered it well–but the elm-grove extended for more than an acre. How could he locate one particular spot in the midst of that profound obscurity?

He took advantage of one shaft of moonlight to move out of the wood, then he set himself to follow the edge of the stand, looking for the little footpath that he had already missed once. A second glimmer of light showed him a dozen petty paths winding into the undergrowth, all very similar. At the same time, he heard the sound of carriage-wheels on the driveway; the guests were going home and the doors would soon be closed. He had to make haste.

Gaston picked one of the footpaths at random and followed it for a hundred paces; it led him straight to an enormous stump surrounded by heaps of dead wood. He retraced his steps at a run and took another route, then another: they both took him deeper into the wood. The lights were being extinguished in the château. It would no longer be possible to leave by the gate.

An entire hour went by while he searched in vain, and Gaston had quite lost heart, when a shaft of moonlight lit a spark at his feet. Something flat and metallic glittered in the brushwood. He bent down, picked up the object that he had previously hidden there, buttoned his coat over his precious find, and made for the wall that enclosed the park.

A stone wall is a small obstacle to a twenty-year-old in good health. He climbed over it easily, without injury to anything but the knees of his trousers and the cuffs of his black coat. I dare say that His Grace's guard-dogs howled a little, but Gaston was already on his way along the highway.

There was an official on duty at the toll-gate, sleeping in that extraordinary fashion which does not prevent officials from seeing confusedly and moving slowly. There are barriers on every road into Paris, whose presence is vital to the taxation of wines and spirits. The somnambulist, seeing a bare-headed man whose trousers were ripped at the knees and whose coat was torn at the cuffs, leapt to the conclusion that he must be a smuggler intent on the fraudulent introduction of a vast quantity of wine, and sounded the alarm in order to rouse his five companions from the same magical sleep. The six functionaries, moved by the best of intentions, demanded that Gaston should either show them his import license or pay his duty.

When Gaston demanded to be allowed through, he was seized and searched, but released again because the officials had found nothing on him but a little missal bound in velvet and enclosed in polished steel, at the end of a length of chain, also made of steel. Gaston, when he saw the missal in the hands of these good men, fell into a chair and almost lost consciousness–but the unanimous opinion of the officials was that even if the object were hollow and full of proof spirit, its capacity was too small for any tax to be payable.

Gaston accepted the return of the missal as if he were taking possession of a treasure and hurried on his way, without bidding farewell to the men in green who had persecuted him while they were lost in a dream.

The missal was, as we have already established, bound in velvet and hermetically encased in steel, sealed by an antique lock; its solidity seemed proven. A large number of ecclesiastics possess breviaries of that sort, but we have no intention of laying a trap for the perspicacity of the reader. The little book was most certainly the one which had formerly hung, attached to a steel chain, around the neck of Monsignor Benedict. Gaston had found it on the ground and picked it up when the Archbishop's guests had left the lawn after the storytelling. But why had he not returned it to Monsignor Benedict? Why, instead, had he hidden it as if he were concealing a treasure? The young and handsome Marquis de Lorgères certainly did not look like a thief.

To tell the truth, it could hardly have been an object of very great importance, since Monsignor Benedict had not even noticed that it was missing during the three hours that the concert had lasted.

Or could it?

It was about two o'clock in the morning when the Marquis arrived at the end of the Rue de l'Université, in front of his mother's townhouse. The de Montfort residence was situated not far from the Bourbon Palace, close to the corner of the Rue de Courty. Gaston did not pause at the impressive gateway; he turned the corner of the Rue de Courty, still running, and rang the doorbell of a modest house which backed on to the rear garden of the mansion.

This simple topographical detail will perhaps explain to the reader the innocent and mute mystery of the sentiments of Gaston and Lenore. Lenore's bedroom window looked out upon the vast garden where Gaston had–for an entire month–been taking endless walks.

The door opened. Gaston went up to the second floor and was introduced by Monsieur d'Arnheim himself into a rather squalid apartment. The little spaniel, Mina, came to welcome her friend.

The silent and somber Monsieur d'Arnheim opened the door of his study and closed it behind them.

The clock on the Bourbon palace was sounding five o'clock when Monsieur d'Arnheim's study-door opened again to let Gaston out. Some agreement must have been reached between them, because they shook hands before parting.

Chapter XI
The Statement of Account

There was a large bowl of punch steaming on the table. It was already half-empty. They were both there: the tall one and the short one.

Baron von Altenheimer was pacing back and forth across the room, with an enormous Prussian pipe clenched in his teeth. His thatch of black hair was gone; this was a tall young man, nearly bald, and what hair he had was reddish-brown. His black coat had been replaced by a Turkish jacket crisscrossed and edged with gold embroidery.

Monsignor Benedict, wearing a crimson satin dressing-gown, was stretched out on an old sofa with a Havana cigar between his lips. Under the dressing-gown the black collar of his clerical garb was visible, the sluggard not having taken the trouble to get out of it. The room was large and high-ceilinged, but it was untidy and ill-furnished. It had two beds. A distinct odor of low-life was in the air.

They both gave every impression of being in a good mood, and there was a brotherly intimacy in their chatter.

"There'll be a big noise in the corridors of power in the morning," the tall one said, laughing.

"Better there than here," replied the short one. "I love the Rue de Richelieu. If I ever settle in Paris for good, I'll treat myself to a house on the corner of the Rue de Richelieu and the boulevard."

"Personally, I prefer that nice house that looks out on the Rue de la Paix," the Baron replied. "I think it's the Osmond house. I must pay my respects there some day...but think of the row we kicked up last night!" He went on laughing.

"You were superb," said the younger brother, insincerely.

"And you were very pretty," the older riposted, "but I must admit that when it comes to dupes, these Parisians are the cream."

"The most spiritual people in the world," Benedict murmured, yawning.

The Baron resumed his pacing. "There were a lot of trinkets in that collection," he went on, disdainfully. "Except for your ring and my snuff-box, I didn't see much apart from the Princess's bracelet..."

"You're telling me," Benedict replied. "Parisians have jewels specially made for collection days."

The Baron smiled and downed a glass of punch in a single draught. He filled up the Monsignor's glass, which had also been drained, albeit in smaller gulps. "We won't get as much as a thousand *louis* for the lot," he said. "Paris is a dump, I tell you."

"For work, certainly... but when one retires from the business..."

"All right then," the elder interrupted, depositing his immense porcelain pipe on the table. "You said it. Let's talk business. It's already one o'clock in the morning and it's scarcely worth going to bed–we have to be on the road to Boulogne by four."

"I'm tired," said the Monsignor, yawning for the second time and stretching lazily on his sofa.

122

"We have to, for safety's sake..."

"Leave off! Who the devil do you expect to winkle us out of here?"

"Stranger things have happened," the tall man said.

"There are two places made for hiding in," the shorter man replied. "Paris and the Black Forest–and Paris is ten times as good as the Black Forest!"

"But you agreed..." said the Baron reproachfully.

"I've changed my mind," Benedict said, dryly.

"You no longer want to leave?"

"Of course... but not tonight."

"Why not?"

"I have my reasons."

"It's foolishness," complained the elder, testily.

"Possibly," the younger replied, "but I'm my own master, and am at liberty to be foolish."

The Baron made an effort to contain the anger that was rumbling within him. "Look here," he said, abruptly but without losing his temper. "What mischief has Satan put into your head? Tell me!"

"Very well, Old William," the Monsignor replied. "I don't want us to fall out over this; there's probably a nice stroke or two to be pulled in London these days. I'll tell you my reasons, just as though you had the right to call me to account. To begin with, we have nothing to fear here; not one of our hirelings knows where we are. No one even knows that English is our mother tongue, since you had the honor of being raised within sight of the Tower of London and I was born in the parish of Saint Giles, not two steps from Oxford Street, where I did my earliest jobs. So, tomorrow morning, we get out of this slum; we go to Vincennes, clean ourselves up in the woods and we come back, arm in arm, to the toll-gate: William Staunton, bookseller of Ave Maria Lane and Mrs. Olivia Staunton, his young companion, both on their first trip to Paris, their pockets full of guineas and determined to have a jolly good time. We come down somewhere in the vicinity of the Palais-Royal–and who'll see what has become of the privy councilor to the King of Wurtemburg and the pope's chamberlain?

"It's absurd," said the older, coldly. "Is that all?"

"No. If you're absolutely determined to be gone, I'll go too–but not till tomorrow evening, and not without Mademoiselle d'Arnheim."

The Baron's pallor gave way to redness. "Do you know who that d'Arnheim girl is?" he murmured, through clenched teeth.

"Of course!" the younger man replied. "It's Lenore...I gave her up for twelve hundred thousand francs when we were poor, but today I'd pay two millions for her... I love her!"

"Imbecile!" said the elder, harshly. "You've risked your life ten times for a few *louis*..."

"I love her, d'you hear?" cried the blond man, raising himself up on his elbow. "I want to carry her off, and I shall! Don't shrug your shoulders like that! It's a long while since you were in command here, Old William. I'm no longer a child; my word counts for just as much as yours."

Old William–seeing that yet another name has been given to Baron von Altenheimer, we might as well use it–crossed his long arms over his breast and said: "You don't suppose, Bobby, that I'd help you to play that sort of game?"

Bobby–which was, perhaps, the Monsignor's true name–replied: "Didn't you help me with the blond girl in Itèbe? And pretty Efflam in Petrovaradin? And the girl in Venice? And the one in Stuttgart? And the rest?

Me, I've always helped you, like the minor player who feeds the cue to Kemble or Talma [25]. I'm as good an actor as you are, William, and you need me more than I need you."

Smiling scornfully, the tall man turned his back and went to refill his glass,

"Just listen," the short man went on, "and you'll see that we both know how to put together a plan of attack. When you donated your pocket-book with the thousand-franc notes–which wasn't bad, I admit–I thought of something better. I went to His Lordship in my turn and said to him: Your Highness, could you tell me where this respectable Monsieur d'Arnheim lives? What could His Highness think but that the fortune of his protégés would be made if we were to go there? I have the address: in the Rue de Courty, at the corner of the Rue de l'Université. Tomorrow, I'll spend half an hour making up my face in the image of a very respectable marquise, fifty or sixty years old. There was just such a one at the Archbishop's; I'll copy her perfectly. I shan't bother to mention the costume, which is a mere bagatelle. Thus transformed into a dowager, I arrive at Monsieur d'Arnheim's house at the hour when society ladies are wont to circulate, in mid-afternoon. Madame la Comtesse de Chastellux... or de Noailles... or de Mortemart... some irresistible name, at any rate... on behalf of the Archbishop of Paris. I go in; I explain that I heard the young and interesting *virtuosa* yesterday at the Château of Conflans. I have a niece... or the daughter of my poor eldest son, who is dead. I have found that she has a natural bent for music, which is not surprising, since her father had such a lovely voice! Would you like to get into my carriage, my dear child? I want to introduce you to my daughter-in-law... in spite of all your skepticism, you can't pretend that there's anything in the least difficult about it. The little one gets in..."

"And you take her all the way to London in one go?" the erstwhile Baron von Altenheimer interrupted, sarcastically.

"You'll allow me to suppose," Monsignor Bobby replied, acidly, "that a boy like me, transformed from a dowager into a great lord, could easily succeed in pleasing a young girl..."

"You'll allow me to suppose," the tall man interrupted again, "that a stupid act is the greatest stupidity of all! Even if it were supposed that a boy like you, a little less highly-born than my boot, is exactly what is required to play the role of Don Juan, I'd still say that it's absurd. Firstly, the Prince might recognize you. Secondly, I don't want to be inconvenienced on our travels by a woman."

The smaller man lay back on his pillow and sent a long plume of smoke spiraling towards the ceiling. "Ripe fruits that one hesitates to pick go bad," he muttered, clenching his teeth. "Between the two of us, I believe the pear is ripe; if we stay together, William, it will go so bad that we'll get it into our heads to cut one another's throats before long."

"I've a mind to..." William began, his voice tremulous and menacing.

"There, you see!" Bobby said, coldly. "The pear's ripe–we must go our separate ways."

The tall man made a determined effort to contain his anger. He drank two glasses of punch in rapid succession, then he said: "All right, then–split us up!"

"The share-out won't be difficult," said Bobby, who seemed much less emotional than his elder partner. "It won't take long. The banknotes are in two lots in the missal. I anticipated that our association wouldn't last forever and I've always taken care to divide them up into wads of equal value."

"Oh, you anticipated that, did you?" William said. "When I found you so poor, and so ragged."

"Were you rich?" Bobby demanded, before adding: "Go on, Old William, we have nothing for which to reproach one another. If you've earned your share, I've deserved twice as much."

"Ungrateful spawn," murmured the tall man. "But you're right—it's time to part... where's the missal?"

Bobby put his cigar between his lips and patted his side beneath the dressing-gown. "Good accounts make good friends," he said. "You should have a statement listing the exact contents of the missal in your pocket-book."

"I have the pocket-book."

"Get it out, so that we can settle up." He was still rummaging among the ample folds of satin. He showed no obvious signs of anxiety.

"Right!" said the tall man.

"Right," Bobby echoed. "I must have put it under my pillow when I came in, as I usually do. Go see."

William crossed the room and snatched the pillow from one of the beds. "There's nothing here," he said. "You have it on you."

Bobby got up. His expression was seized by a vague dread. Instead of continuing to pat the satin of his dressing-gown, he tore it from his body, to gain better access to the costume which he had worn at the Arch-bishop's soirée. Both hands groped about his left side. He became very pale and his cigar fell from his lips. William, who was following him with a determined stare, was red in the face but he said not a word.

They moved towards one another, each now clutching an open blade produced from who knows where. They came face to face in the middle of the room, looking deep into one another's eyes as if to read the minds behind them, and they said with one voice, through gritted teeth: "You've stolen the missal!"

Bobby tried to duck under William's thrust, while William swayed backwards in the attempt to avoid Bobby's. Then they set themselves on guard again, standing toe to toe, the long face of the taller looming over the blond head of the smaller. Bobby's neck was bleeding and there was a red stain in William's armpit; both thrusts had struck home.

They paused for a moment thus, their left hands splayed before their breasts, ready to parry, while their right hands trembled as they gripped their daggers tightly. Both men obviously knew enough about the art of fencing to concentrate on protecting the head and the heart, leaving the limbs to take their chances–it doesn't matter much if one is wounded there, provided that one kills one's opponent. Each of them knew that he would have to sacrifice a little blood of his own to purchase a full measure of the other's.

Their eyes shone like four red-hot coals. Perhaps William seemed stronger, but Bobby was the more terrible. On seeing them both inflamed by rage and intent on murder, one would have bet on the knife of Ange the vampire against the dagger of the Chevalier Ténèbre.

William was the first to drop his weapon, having first taken a step back. Bobby lowered his arms, saying: "You're scared, and you're going to give back the missal!"

"I'm not scared," the tall man replied, "but I can see that the chain is still around your neck. You haven't stolen it–you've lost it!"

"Lost it!" cried Bobby. "The chain is pure steel. It would carry a hundred books."

"Yes," the other interrupted, while seizing a loose end of the chain. "It's broken!"

Bobby dropped his knife in his turn.

"Right by the rivet," he murmured. "But how was it that I didn't feel the absence of the weight? I know! I remember! On the lawn, I pulled on the chain and it resisted..." He jerked violently at the other end of the chain, which detached itself from the material of his vestment.

"A flaw," he stammered. "And the broken link was caught up in the fold of my costume."

William took the chain, while Bobby, who had froth at the corners of his mouth, closed his fist and said: "I bought that chain in Frankfurt, at number three the Zeil. I'll make an express trip to Frankfurt to tear that shopkeeper's heart out."

They knew only too well that they had both made a mistake. Neither could maintain their suspicions in the face of that mute witness, the broken chain. They were now entirely given over to consternation.

William took one end of the chain in each hand and pulled them apart with all his strength; the chain remained solid.

"It only had the one flaw," he murmured.

His pocket-book was on the table, ready to verify the count. He opened it and began to read in a faint voice: "Two banknotes of fifty thousand pounds... number one... two million five hundred thousand francs!"

"The Bank of England only took five impressions from the plate," Bobby sighed, "and we had two of them."

"Number two," the tall man went on, "two banknotes of a thousand pounds... Number three, two banknotes of a thousand pounds... Number four, two banknotes of a thousand pounds..."

"There were a hundred of them" Bobby interrupted him.

"Another two million five hundred thousand francs! Number one hundred and two, two banknotes of five thousand pounds... that was after the Venice job... Number one hundred and three, from the same job, two banknotes of four thousand pounds... Number one hundred and four..."

Bobby threw himself on the pocket-book, tearing it from William's grasp, and pressed it tightly between his hands.

"We had millions!" said the tall man, collapsing in a fit of tears. "Millions and millions and millions..."

"Millions and millions and millions!" echoed the small man, grinding his teeth like a tiger.

They were still looking at one another.

"Shall we kill one another?" Bobby said, coldly.

William picked up the punch-bowl in both hands and drank down its remaining contents in one draught. Then he drew himself proudly up to his full height and he too said: "Shall we kill one another?"

But Bobby had already put his blade away. He began to pace back and forth across the room. William let himself fall into a chair. There was a long silence.

"Brother," said the short man, in the end, "you said it a little while ago: we've often risked our lives for a few *louis*."

"Do you have a plan?" William asked, his eyes calm and clear now.

"There are two possibilities, brother. Either the missal is still on the lawn, in the place where it fell, or one of the Archbishop's guests picked it up."

"That's true."

"We must not forget that in either case the missal is secured by a secret catch that would defy the most skilful of locksmiths."

"I believe so."

"We have two more parts to play: one on the grassy stage, the other in the bedroom of the man–whoever it might be–who had the misfortune to find the missal."

They took one another by the hand and said in unison, in a low voice: "He's a dead man!"

Chapter XII
The Princess Gets Up

Shortly before dawn the dogs guarding the Château de Conflans began to howl. It is a matter of record that the Archbishop's guests got little sleep that night. At four o'clock in the morning, or thereabouts, two men–one tall and one short–climbed over the wall and went into the woods. They wore the costumes of working men, but they were both well-armed beneath their shirts.

Dawn, when it broke, found them in the clearing where the friends of the Archbishop of Paris had gathered as night fell on the previous evening. They were both crawling on the grass, searching the shadows with their eyes.

"We won't find it," said the tall one, abruptly rising to his feet.

"Why's that?" the shorter one demanded.

"Because someone got here before us."

"What makes you think...?"

"Get your bearings, now that it's not as dark," William replied. "I am on the exact spot where you were standing as I finished my story, and my foot is where the missal fell."

"Should have fallen."

"Did fall," the tall man insisted. He pointed a finger at the grass between his feet.

The smaller man approached, got down on his knees and leaned over the designated spot. He could clearly see the bruised grass–and beneath it, the imprint cut into the soil by the sudden arrest of a rectangular object. He immediately got to his feet.

The two brothers, without saying a word, redirected their steps towards the wall of the park. The first part had been played, and the game lost; the second had yet to begin.

As they approached the wall, William suddenly stopped, saying: "Someone else came this way last night."

Bobby's educated eyes were already examining a section of the wall whose tapestry of ivy had been disturbed. The broken shoots had not had time to go yellow, and the detached foliage was still fresh.

"A scrap of cloth!" he cried.

"Fine cloth," said William. "That never belonged to the clothing of some night-prowler. Look at these tracks!"

The footprints left by the Marquis were, indeed, visible on the dewy ground.

"Dancing-shoes," William went on. "A foot like a woman's!"

Bobby climbed in car-like fashion to the top of the wall, where something white was lodged.

"G. L. and the crown of a marquis!" he cried, throwing a handkerchief to William.

"Gaston de Lorgères!" murmured William. "Why didn't he leave the château by the main gate?" He climbed the wall in his turn.

The two of them took the road to Paris, pensively.

"Anything under your shirts?" asked the guard at the toll-gate.

William stopped, as an idea came into his head. Striking the pose, innocent and astute at the same time, of a concerned citizen, he said instead of answering the question: "Are you also responsible for arresting thieves?"

"Why do you ask?" the official countered, while patting the tall man's shirt in a tokenistic fashion.

"Because it's my opinion that our thief must have come this way."

The official, three-quarters awakened by curiosity, said: "What thief?"

"The sharp dresser who was carrying Monsieur le curé's brand-new breviary, that's who!"

"Well, I never!" exclaimed the man at the toll-gate. "There's a turn up!"

He said this in such a manner that sweat immediately sprang up on William's and Bobby's foreheads. Their hearts beat faster. They said, as one: "You got him!"

"He had no duty to pay," the official retorted, stoutly, "and I'm no gendarme."

"What time was it when he came through?" William asked, sadly.

"An hour after midnight... he'll be a long way off by now, if he's still running."

Later that morning, an impoverished old woman took up a position in the Rue de Courty, not far from the house where Monsieur d'Arnheim lived, while an unfamiliar beggar established himself on a step facing the house occupied by the Princess de Montfort.

This occurred some considerable time before the Princess, whose sleep was prolonged by the emotions and exertions of the previous night, was ready to face the new day. Her first words, after waking up. were an enquiry as to Gaston's whereabouts.

"Monsieur le Marquis," her chambermaid replied, "has already presented himself three times asking to speak to Madame la Princesse."

"It couldn't be helped, Justine. I feel weak, and I haven't the strength to get up to receive him. Tell him to come in."

An instant later, Gaston was introduced into his mother's bedroom.

"My dear child," the Princess said to him at once, "You know me, and you know that I don't like to scold. Today, when even I might be inclined to reprimand you, I shall abstain, because I want you to trust me, to trust me absolutely. Something extraordinary has happened to you; I know that. Would you like to make your confession to me?"

"With all my heart, mother," the young Marquis replied, kissing her hand tenderly. "It is precisely for the purpose of telling you what is happening to me that I have taken the liberty of demanding an interview with you this morning."

"Then I shall listen, Gaston, asking only one thing of you: that you are perfectly frank with the mother who loves you."

The Marquis blushed slightly, but he replied without hesitation: "You might well complain about me, Madame, but not of any lack of frankness. I want to marry."

The Princess reeled from the blow, taking cover beneath her bedclothes. The timid Gaston had gone for good, it seemed.

"I must point out," the lady replied, her eyebrows furrowing in spite of herself, "that you are a child, in love for the first time, and that you have gone mad."

It seemed that Gaston was prepared for that kind of reaction, for he lifted his mother's hand to his lips again.

"To marry a singer...!" the Princess began, angrily.

"Permit me, Madame," Gaston interrupted her, very softly. "I hope to furnish proof in the course of this con-versation...I am in love, as you have done me the honor of observing, in the second place. I admit that much. As for having gone mad, it's said that such is the lot of lively minds illuminated by superabundant imagination; in my mind and my conscience I feel that I am out of reach of that danger–I am not at all well-endowed for going mad. If my cool, practical and prosaic character has no other advantage, it protects me from that..."

"Oh, get on with it!" the Princess cried, impatiently.

"Which brings us to the singer, Madame, and since you have asked me to be frank, I will admit, frankly, that I am astonished and wounded by that insinuation. I have long attained the age when such pranks are played, and I have noticed that the stubborn regularity of my conduct has occasioned a certain mockery among my friends. I believe I can even affirm that it has sometimes put a smile on my mother's lips..."

"Oh, Gaston...!"

"My God, Madame, youth which does not pass, as it is said, is entitled to raise a smile... I have been living like a little saint. On the other hand, no crisis or malady, chivalrous or romantic, has ever troubled my existence, which has been as peaceful as the lovely little stream that winds through your park at Chelles–which you yourself have bitterly reproached for having neither a waterfall nor a whirlpool... Were I not a de Montfort, I

136

would say that I had good bourgeois blood in my veins, retaining from the first of January to Saint Sylvester's day [26] the moderate and calm temperature of mediocrity..."

"What case are you pleading now?" the Princess interrupted him, raising her eyes. "You're like a Norman lawyer this morning. Are you starting your diplomatic career with me?"

"I have renounced diplomacy, Madame," Gaston replied, calmly. "My vocation is to make a rich marriage and to live on my estates."

"A rich marriage!" echoed the stupefied Princess. "Your cousin Emerance has fifty thousand francs a year."

"My mother might perhaps have been able to deduce," Gaston replied, lifting the Princess's hand to his lips for the third time, "that if I have not shown overmuch eagerness in the matter of that union, it is because I have another, more important, party in mind."

Madame de Montfort rubbed her eyes with her knuckles. She suspected that she was not yet fully awake.

"More important!" she repeated, perhaps more shocked by the manner of the expression than the idea itself. "Are you really there, my boy?"

"I believe that I have been unkindly judged thus far, Mother," Gaston replied, "and my preamble, which may have seemed overlong to you, can hardly have modified your opinion on that score. I can only do myself justice by telling you that I am a respectful son, obedient and loving—but marriage, Madame, is one's entire future!"

"I have never tried to force you..." the Princess began.

"Of course, Mother, of course—but do you imagine that you had not made it clear what path your maternal affection wished me to take? My cousin Emerance..."

"Say no more, I beg you, about your cousin Emerance, Gaston! Your cousin Emerance was not an accessory to the building of my beautiful castles in Spain. I don't even know if we would have been able to obtain her hand."

"I don't know either, Madame, and I don't care. It is in Hungary, not in Spain, that I have built my own imaginary castles." He stopped, as if a vision had suddenly taken hold of him.

The Princess looked at him, open-mouthed. "And what connection have you ever had with Hungary?" she asked, after a pause.

"You have forgotten, Madame," Gaston replied, "that you commissioned me, some time ago, to take steps to withdraw your interest from the property at Debrecen owned by my brother the Duc."

"And you met the daughter of some local magnate in the lawyer's office?"

"I implore you, Madame, not to make fun," the young Marquis said, seriously. "there was never a subject less suitable for joking... Do you remember the story told last night by the Baron von Altenheimer?"

The Princess clapped her hands together. "I knew that there was some extravagance under all this!" she cried. "I suppose it concerns the lovely Lenore, daughter of Prince Jacobyi."

"You are right, Madame," said Gaston, unblinkingly.

"What an evening!" the Princess went on. "I dreamed of those cunning scoundrels all night. I refused to believe their silly story as a matter of principle...

138

Look, Gaston, all joking aside, I want to talk to you seriously..."

"Does the party not seem suitable to you, Mother?..." asked the young Marquis, his calmness put to the test.

"What party? Are we going back to the vampires of yesteryear and that stupid phantasmagoria? Don't talk to me about marrying the Sleeping Beauty or some other fairy tale. Stop now, Monsieur le Marquis, or you'll have me convinced that your mind is definitely unhinged."

"Madame," said Gaston, unhurriedly, "Hungary is not Fairyland. Our cousin Camille, Prince of Guéménée and de Rochefort, was married only last year to the Princess of Wertheim-Rosenberg, and we ourselves are descended from the ancient kings of Hungary through Charlotte de Croy d'Havré, my great-grandmother on my father's side."

The Princess took her flask, opened it, closed it again, then opened it again so that she could close it again. In every country where there are flasks, such gestures indicate the exhaustion of patience.

"I suppose," the Marquis continued, redoubling his persuasive efforts, "that any teller of fantastic tales, whether honest man or bandit, might take the name de Montfort–which you wear so well, Mother dear–and introduce it into his tale like the one we heard yesterday. Would that prevent you from being at the head of a noble French family? Madame, I beseech you to believe that the information I have does not come from Baron von Altenheimer–if that really is his name. I am speaking seriously of serious matters, and I have come to ask you whether you are willing to approach Prince Jacobyi on my behalf to ask for the hand of his daughter in marriage."

If the Princess had been standing up, she would have fallen down.

"This is too much, Monsieur le Marquis!" she said, sitting up straight again. Then she added, in a sarcastic tone: "And to what part of the world would it be necessary to address the letter to this Oedipus, soliciting the hand of his Antigone?"

"I would not have dared to compare the one that I love to the saintly figure bequeathed to us by antique poetry," Gaston replied, still perfectly placid. "The letter must be addressed to Chrétien Baszin, Prince Jacobyi, at Chandor Castle, near Szeged, Hungary."

The Princess opened her eyes wide. "Gaston," she murmured, "is there really something at the bottom of all this?"

"I don't know how to convince you of that elementary truth," the Marquis replied, "except to assure you that there is a young lady who will be your daughter-in-law and who will bring me a dowry of five or six hundred thousand francs a year."

"This is so extraordinary!" murmured the Princess. "You have said not a word to me before today!"

"I confess, Madame, that I have only been a man for twenty-four hours."

"You cannot hope, however," said Madame de Montfort, in a tone which was already much changed, "that I will embark upon an enterprise of this sort without explanations and proofs."

"Mother," replied Gaston, solemnly and sincerely, "I will give you clear and precise explanations–but as for proofs, it will be necessary to content yourself with the word of honor of a man who has never told a lie."

"Is it your own word of honor?"

"It is my own word of honor, Madame."

"I will listen, my son. Remember the name that you bear, and what indignity and cowardice there would be in deceiving your mother."

Gaston set out, briefly and clearly, the provisions of Hungarian legislation regarding matters of litigation.

All princesses have some understanding of the language of business. Let us not be deceived; only those possessed of considerable fortunes are elevated to such a condition, and that prose is the very soil in which the poetry of grandeur flourishes. The Princess de Montfort understood readily enough the mechanism by which feudal rights could be repurchased: a powerful instrument, which is not as insolently injurious to the idea of progress as the principle of inalienability or the right of primogeniture, but which works usefully and ceaselessly to consolidate great territorial domains.

"Chrétien Baszin, Prince Jacobyi," Gaston continued, "having been dispossessed at the end of 1821, has until the end of 1826 to buy back his estates, at the same price at which they were sold, without any regard to any further or partial sales which have taken place since then. That is the law. So much the worse for those who have taken advantage of the same law! Prince Jacobyi, profiting from the benevolence of the law, has bought back his castle and his lands, which are as vast as a province."

"Has bought back?" the Princess repeated. "The deal is done, and completed, is it not? You can assure me of that, under oath?"

"I assure you, under oath, Mother," the young Marquis replied, firmly, "that the magnate Jacobyi will receive your request at Chandor Castle, of which he will be the sole and sovereign master. I assure you, under oath, that if I introduce Lenore into your house, it will be as Princess Jacobyi, sole heir to her father's immense fortune."

Everything had now been said. The Princess remained silent and Gaston allowed her time to reflect. We shall take advantage of the pause to admit to the reader that, given the character of Madame de Montfort–who was otherwise a most excellent and charming princess– Gaston had chosen, with devastating tact, the only route which could possibly have won her consent. He had played the part of the money-lover so admirably that the first words his mother spoke were: "I fear, in truth–yes, my child, I fear–that the idea of a fortune... in marriage, believe me, a fortune is not everything!"

"I like a fortune, Madame."

"Undoubtedly, but the wife herself..."

"But I adore the wife, who is an angel!"

"Very well, Gaston. Ring for my chambermaid. I want to get up. We shall see... we shall think on it..."

Instead of ringing the bell, Gaston went to the sideboard to pick up one of those ornamental rosewood boxes called *papeteries*. He placed the charming object on the coverlet in front of his mother. It contained blue ink (which princesses and Doctor Récamier love, although I hate it myself), Surrey paper as glossy as satin, a steel pen–the first one, invented by Perry–and Spanish wax that exhaled a light and temperate perfume. Gaston opened the dainty desk, arranged the pad of paper and dipped the Perry pen into the blue ink.

"I have rivals," he murmured, "and time is pressing."

If he had done as others do; if he had put his head upon his mother's bosom, saying only: "I love..." Who knows? Perhaps it would have worked as well. We are describing what actually happened.

The Princess, who was a woman of style, wrote a dignified and concise letter, perfectly polite but getting straight to the point. She was paid in full, for Gaston hugged her as if she were some poor woman of the suburbs and as if he, the Marquis, were wearing the shirt of some Parisian urchin. Such extravagant gestures of affection, proscribed by etiquette, are nevertheless well worth having.

Gaston fled with his prey. We cannot say for sure whether he noticed the beggar sitting on the step facing the main gate of the de Montfort house, or the poor old lady stationed across from the house where Monsieur and Mademoiselle d'Arnheim were living. He could have seen both of them, for he went directly from the grand gate to the humble door on the Rue de Courty. What cannot be doubted is that the beggar and the poor old lady saw him; they abandoned their posts instantly, meeting at the corner of the two streets and exchanging several words in a low tone.

Gaston did not stay more than a quarter of an hour in Monsieur d'Arnheim's house. He came out, his face radiant, and went on foot towards the Rue de Lille. The beggar walked behind him, while the poor woman went back to her sentry-duty. The beggar returned an hour later and said to the old woman: "He's ordered a carriage."

"When for?"

"I don't know... let's wait for nightfall."

At five o'clock, Gaston returned to the townhouse in a cab. As he passed the threshold of the gateway, the beggar went towards the old woman and said: "He's going in to dinner. We have an hour to do likewise."

They went off together. They were gone for no more than five minutes, but it was too much.

Every sentinel knows that he must have a very good reason to abandon his post. The Marquis had not, in fact, gone in to dinner. He could have been seen coming out again a few moments later, on horseback, and turning once again into the Rue de Courty. A carriage and horses drew up before Monsieur d'Arnheim's house, and Monsieur d'Arnheim came out in his travelling clothes to take his place in the carriage. The driver whipped his horses into motion and Gaston galloped alongside.

The carriage went right through Paris and made its exit through the toll-gate at La Villette, then took the Strasbourg Road. Gaston maintained his escort over a considerable distance; darkness had fallen when he turned back.

In the meantime, the beggar and the old woman had taken up their posts again and continued their vigil. At about six o'clock, the old woman went to find the beggar. "The Devil with this!" she said.

"Wait," the other replied. patiently, in a deep baritone voice. "The time will come and the place suits our purpose. There's not so much as a stray cat in the Rue de l'Université. We can sit down now on either side of the door."

Scarcely had they taken their places on benches of the kind which are set at the entrances of a great many townhouses in the Faubourg Saint-Germain than the hoofbeats of a horse were heard in the distance. The ragged couple paid no attention to the noise; it was not a horseman that they were waiting for.

The horseman approached and stopped directly in front of the closed gate. The beggar and the old woman stayed in their corners until the moment when the horseman cried out, in an imperious voice: "The gate!" Then they started, both as one.

They leapt to their feet, and a second bound carried each of them to one side of the horse. Gaston was seized by both legs, dragged to the ground, stabbed and searched from head to toe within the blink of an eye.

"Nothing!" said the beggar.

"Nothing," echoed the old woman, with a curse.

The gate opened. The old woman and the beggar took to their heels and, while still in full flight, threw off their rags. One could then have seen, under the next street-lamp, two men running with equal rapidity: one tall, one short.

As for Gaston, the servants who came to open the gate found him bathed in his own blood beside his motionless horse. His breast had been pierced by two thrusts of a dagger.

Chapter XIII
The Black Graves

The Marquis de Lorgères was confined to his bed for four months by his wounds. The thrusts had been masterly; either might have been fatal, and Dupuytren [27] was able to boast for many years afterwards of that particular cure. In the meantime, Prince Jacobyi's reply arrived in Paris–bearing the address of Chandor Castle–and was favorable.

As one would expect, the Princess, although she trusted the Marquis's word completely, had not been deterred from obtaining information from her cousins the de Rohans, who were established in Hungary. It was, after all, part of her duty as a mother. The information thus transmitted was, like the Prince's reply, favorable.

The Prince had bought back his lands. The Prince was, as before, one of the greatest lords of the Austrian Empire.

The marriage of the Marquis de Lorgères to Princess Lenore took place in Szeged, at the beginning of March 1826.

Early in April that same year, a little old man with a pleasant face and an easy-gong manner was trudging along the high road from Pest to Szeged, pulling a handcart containing a poor creature who looked like a living corpse and who had, moreover, lost his reason. Not far from Szeged, upstream of Morzau, there is a spring whose water is clear, protected by a little minaret from the dust of the road. The water of that spring was blessed by Saint Miklos, and has the power to cure madness. The little old man was a good father who had come from the region of Ofen, dragging his unfortunate son every step of the way.

Since that era, our French engineers have laid four parallel iron bars all the way from Pest to Belgrade, via Szeged. It only requires a few hours to cross that vast plain. The last time I saw Szeged, that strange town which contains as many bells as the entire district of Beauce [28], it had an old pupil of our *Ecole Polytechnique* for its king. He was in the process of building a four thousand-feet bridge across the Tisza: a magnificent bridge to carry the railway. Austrian engineers came to study the work, carried out by a human ant-hive in which one could identify twenty races and whose members spoke fifteen languages.

I realized then that the confusion of languages had counted for nothing in preventing the erection of the Tower of Babel. The bridge marched upon the waters, so to speak, supported by great tubular columns, and I saw a daguerreotype machine with the round eye of its black chamber already focused on its arches. This is our future civilization–but on that same voyage I saw accused and condemned men, stretched out entirely naked on the damp earth in the cellars of Turkish forts: forts whose walls, flanked by corpulent towers, looked over that same Parisian bridge. We have, however, already raised the possibility that men might break out of prisons, even those whose stones have been set permanently in place.

In 1826, the high road entered the city via a lake of mud in winter, a sea of dust in summer. The dust of Szeged is famous in Hungary, and the mud too. Ingenious Magyars set planks end to end in order that these precipices may be crossed, but the regulations require carriages to pass alongside them lest they be rendered useless, and the trusting pedestrian who dares to set foot upon them is almost certain to fall off.

The pious father, the hand-cart and the son arrived two hours before sunset at the horribly churned-up plain called the Place Joseph II, in the shadow of the beautiful Byzantine Church of Saint Job. The hand-cart stopped in front of a sort of caravanserail, bearing a sign depicting a saint clad in red, whose interior courtyard, as large as one of our public squares, was bordered by worm-eaten wooden arcades. The little old man asked politely for the least expensive room in the inn, deposited his son there and went out to get his papers stamped by a government official. His passport bore the name Petroz Aszuth, leather-merchant of Kaiserbad.

The servants in Hungarian inns are usually Slavs and, in consequence, almost as garrulous as the staff of French taverns. Before dinner was served, everyone knew the whole story of little Petroz Aszuth, who was taking his idiot son to the spring of Saint Miklos. The poor *lumpen* boy was certainly in great need of the spring. The innkeeper's daughter who took him his food was kind enough to strike up a conversation with him to relieve his boredom slightly, but she returned saying: "One might as well talk to Schwartz, the guard-dog!"

The night was already well-advanced when the little old man came back. He did not want any supper and immediately went up to his room. As soon as he was inside, he locked the door and drew the curtains over the window.

The idiot leapt from his bed and put on a blond wig. You would have immediately recognized the long lean

148

figure of Baron von Altenheimer. "Do you know something, Bobby?" he asked, animatedly.

Bobby removed his dirty beard, which was making his rosy cheeks itch, and plunged his face into a basin of fresh water, displaying the pretty face of Monsignor Benedict.

"Well," he said, "this place hasn't changed–they still chatter like magpies. I know the story from beginning to end."

Tall William sat down on the foot of his bed to smoke his porcelain pipe. "Go on," he said.

"It was the Marquis all right," Bobby replied, lighting his cigar. "He's given the missal to old Jacobyi, who's bought his hovel back..."

"Then they're thieves like us!" William cried. "The missal only had five hundred thousand florins of his, from Lenore's ransom, and he'd have needed six times that to buy his estates back!"

Bobby shrugged his shoulders. "If they'd kept the lot," he replied, "I could almost have forgiven them–after all, it's every man for himself, isn't it? But since old Baszin got back his castle, his forests, his lakes and his fields, he's taken out all his mortgages again and borrowed exactly the same sum as the excess he took from the missal. Even before he celebrated the marriage of his daughter, he had delivered our cash into the hands of the Primate of Hungary, the Archbishop of Graz. The fact has been advertised in Vienna, Venice, Stuttgart, Paris and everywhere else, and all the sheep that we have fleeced have turned up, demanding their wool! Pillaged, all of it! Not a single florin of our little hoard remains– and if there were anything left, the rogues would still be queuing up!"

"Wretches!" William groaned.

"Let me tell you," Bobby went on, "everyone is talking about us here. Since we've done what we came to do, we'd best be on our way. They know everything! The story of our Paris venture has become legendary. The tale of the Archbishop's collection is all the rage. And the missal itself... but it's the story of the missal that I want to tell you. The Marquis was running an errand for his mother when he picked up the missal. His intention was to return it to me, but the missal had fallen so unluckily that the secret catch had been sprung. Nothing was broken, but the steel casement could be opened as easily as one might open a book. The Marquis did exactly that, perhaps by chance, and the two fifty-thousand-pound banknotes leapt to his eyes. He understands English, and you had taken care to acquaint him, a few minutes earlier, with the story of the father of Lenore, with whom he was already in love even though he had never spoken to her..."

"I remember!" murmured William. "He had the nerve to ask me for information about rights of repurchase, on the pretext that his brother had property in Debrecen..."

"When he asked you for that information, his plan was conceived," Bobby went on. "He's a smart fellow and I won't regret the bullet that smashes his head."

William took a flat square bottle from his overcoat, which contained brandy. He took a big gulp. "Ever since that business," he said, "we've been unable to get back on our feet. All our capers have gone wrong, in London, in Berlin, in Vienna–he's the cause of all our misfortune!" He passed the bottle to Bobby, who drank before repeating: "He's the cause of all our misfortune!"

"When we've bled him dry, he must die!"

"He must die!" Bobby echoed, again. "I have all the necessary information. They talk of little else in Szeged, because of the story of the missal, which has been on everyone's lips. He's spending his honeymoon at Chandor. He hunts and he fishes. A big hunt is planned for tomorrow."

"We'll be there!" snarled William.

"We'll be there. We must be up early–let's get some sleep, Old William."

The next morning, before daybreak, the little old man from Kaiserbad hitched himself up to his vehicle and carted his maniac son off towards the welcoming spring. The staff of the inn were most impressed by the conduct of the little old man; they pointed him in the right direction and wished him good luck.

The way to the spring was the road to Chandor Castle. After an hour's march, at the moment when dawn silvered the horizon, the hand-cart reached the vast forests of the Baszin domain.

The old man left the main road and pushed the hand-cart into a dense wood. The invalid son, suddenly recovering the agility appropriate to one of his age, leapt on to the moss and opened the false bottom of the cart, from which he extracted two double-barreled shotguns and two costumes of the kind worn by Czech peasants. The change of clothes was affected in no time, and the cart hidden under a bush.

It was not a moment too soon. In the distance, the sound of horns could already be heard.

That day, the Marquis de Lorgères heard several gunshots fired from cover while he was chasing a wild boar. One shot hissed past his ear, and so that he might be certain that he had not been the victim of an illusion, another bullet lodged itself in the material of his hunting-jacket.

But William and Bobby had said it: fortune was against them.

They were found and recognized, and had to show their pursuers a clean pair of heels. When they came to recover their hand-cart and their disguises, they found that the cache had been looted. The road of retreat was closed to them; they could not resume their roles in Szeged.

They spent the night in the woods, resolved to flee; their enterprise had failed. They knew that by the following day the news of their presence would spread throughout the land with lightning rapidity. As soon as they could, they had to put the Tisza between themselves and the crusade that their old misdeeds would launch against them.

"We'll come back later!" William said.

"There'll be a time when Lenore is alone in the castle," Bobby added.

Arriving at the edge of the forest, they saw shadows moving along the river-bank. They had presumed too much in thinking that they had a night to spare; the crusade had already taken up its arms.

They were two determined and tireless individuals, a small army in their own right. They were both fit and they knew the territory well. They conferred for a few minutes and decided to take on the hunt while darkness could provide cover for their flight. The choice of direction was vital; now that the Tisza crossing was closed to them, they could either retrace their steps towards Szeged, then push on towards Kolocza and the Danube, or go upstream to Czongrad, where there was a pontoon bridge.

They decided on the latter course and dived straight into the forest. The night was very dark, which was in their favor.

At two o'clock in the morning, they arrived at the Czongrad bridge, at the moment when the moon–which was in its last quarter–showed its pale and narrow crescent above the horizon.

While they were crossing the bridge unhindered, already congratulating themselves at this first success, they saw boats coming swiftly up the watercourse; at the same time, they heard the muffled sound of hoofbeats made by horses coming along the bank they had just quit.

Was it the Devil himself who had put their enemies on their track?

The moon illuminated them, and their path was discovered.

"Fire!" cried a voice, which came from the nearest boat. They realized immediately that it was old Baszin in person.

They ducked down just in time to avoid a volley of shots which passed over their heads.

The horses on the bank took to the gallop and their hooves were soon drumming on the planks of the bridge.

William and Bobby, desperately accelerating their pace, had reached the other bank. They threw themselves into the cornfields which covered the whole plain between the Tisza and Turkeve. There, they cowered like two partridges in a furrow, getting their breath back.

The cavalcade was already in the field and the cornstalks rattled, shaken by the passage of the horses. There was one moment when the two fugitives had pursuers to the right and left of them, in front of them and behind–but then the hunt passed by.

The foot of the rearmost horse touched William's head, but he stifled a gasp and kept silent. Its rider was Chrétien Baszin, Prince Jacobyi, who had disembarked on the bank and rejoined his galloping horsemen. "Form up in fours!" he cried to those who were ahead of him. "The wretches have made two attempts to assassinate my son-in-law! They shall not escape! Close ranks and beat thoroughly!"

The sounds gradually retreated into the northeast, in the direction of Turkeve. William and Bobby recovered and took a new course, this time heading towards Timisoara, whose wild landscape was almost certain to provide them with adequate shelter. But the horsemen were beating the fields in a zigzag fashion and from time to time our fugitives were obliged to turn aside from their path. Day broke when they were crossing a second river at a ford, below the town of Ghila, which was situated on an island. There was no further shelter thereafter but the tall cornfields of the Great Hungarian Plain.

They were tortured by fatigue, and it was necessary for them to cross a large open space, but chance had put some distance between themselves and the hunt for the time being.

"We must make the most of the last few minutes of darkness," William said. "One last effort!"

They hurled themselves forward, running in a straight line towards the cornfields. On attaining the edge of that ocean of verdure, they looked back in order to scan the ground they had covered. No one was in sight: the hunters had lost their trail. They ran on into the young cornstalks like stags plunging into a forest. After taking a few paces more, they threw themselves on the ground, utterly exhausted, pressing their burning faces to the fresh earth.

"I couldn't have taken another step to save my life!" said Bobby, in a choked voice.

William consulted his watch. "We've been on the run for eleven hours," he said, "and we've covered more than twenty leagues [29]."

"Do we have time to rest?"

"The sun's coming up. In broad daylight they'll soon pick up our trail."

"You're very calm," murmured Bobby.

"Because I'm certain that I can still save myself," William replied.

"How's that?"

"In ten minutes, we can be back in the graves!"

"The graves!" cried Bobby, leaping triumphantly to his feet, no longer feeling fatigued.

The day brightened and the hunters found their trail again. They followed the fresh tracks which cut across the fields of the Great Hungarian Plain at the gallop. They were certain now of their quarry. For the Chevalier Ténèbre and brother Ange, the vampire, to escape it would be necessary for the earth to open beneath them and swallow them!

The hunters went on and on, guided by their master, Prince Jacobyi. At a certain place, though, the tracks became confused, tangled like a ball of string–and then there was nothing.

The earth had indeed opened up and swallowed them. There was no doubt about it.

Chapter XIV
The Tall One and the Short One

September came again. One stormy day, the sun shone on the flat country to the east of Paris, near the confluence of the Marne and the Seine, where two or three more factory-chimneys were smoking.

A train of bundled wooden logs and barges laden with barrels drifted sadly down the river, bound for Bercy, as gloomy as a wine-cellar–but one which contained, in its casks and bottles, novels, sword-thrusts and vaudevilles, Regency rendezvous and songs in honor of the God of good souls, the poetry of the boudoir and the barrier, spirits of every quality, the laughter and smiles of old age for the young and of youth for the old, extravagances for everyone; in sum, all the joy–true and false, sincere and adulterated–which maintains for three hundred and sixty days of every year the chronic folly of the Parisian Carnival! Jean Raisin, elder son of Suresnes, licensed inhabitant of Courtille, has dethroned Bacchus, who is too gentlemanly a god [30].

I once had a nightmare in which I saw Homer revived, with scarlet pimples on the end of his nose. I asked him for news of Achilles, Hector and Agamemnon; he replied that Bordeaux, Mâcon, Epernay, Beaune, Lunel, Cognac and Montpellier had disputed one day the honor of having shown him the light, and that he had written, between two barrelfuls, the twenty-four songs of the Berciad.

This is the repulsive underside of our century: this insulting odor of bad wine, mingled with the noxious fumes of poetic tobacco-smoke, which is all the rage.

When evening came, white dresses were again to be seen here and there on the lawns of the Conflans park beside the Seine, grouped as if in flower-beds. As on the day on which our story began, Archbishop de Quélen was holding a charitable soirée, and the exact parity of circumstance spares us the necessity of elaborate description. The scenery was the same and the guest-list was almost identical. The Bishop of Hermopolis, now as before, was to deliver a short speech, and the same singer–yes, the very same, although she had changed her name to Madame la Marquise Lenore de Lorgères–had been engaged to perform at the concert. She was there, as lovely as youth and happiness, under the wing of the Princess de Montfort, her mother-in-law.

You must certainly have seen, at some time in your life, some pretty little girl, excited by her love for some brand new doll. There is nothing offensive in the comparison; that is exactly how the Princess was in respect of her charming daughter-in-law–quite mad, in effect, with all the liveliness and joyousness that kind of madness brings. She was ten years old again; she had a constant need to smile and caress. The pretty Madame de Maillé let slip at one point: "If that were not my aunt, who has the authority of a princess, I would say that her wheedling ways were in very bad taste." But that was unjust; it is always necessary that good taste should permit good humor.

At dusk, a few drops of rain put all the dresses, white or not, to flight. They took refuge in the hall, where the chairs were already set out for the concert.

It would have been impossible, given the place, the people and the similitude of the setting, to prevent memories resurfacing.

"I hope," said the Doctor, who was still enthusiastically prescribing affusions of cold water taken in warm baths, "that His Lordship the Bishop of Hermopolis will put the produce of his collection in a safe place this time."

"Oh!" the cry went up. "The brothers Ténèbre are not here this evening!"

I cannot deny that a slight shiver of apprehension was manifest here and there in the audience. More than one gaze turned involuntarily towards the entrance-door, beside which Baron von Altenheimer, with his long pale face, and Monsignor Benedict–one tall and one short, the oupire and the vampire–had installed themselves on that eventful night so long ago.

"I wonder what became of those two bold adventurers?" said the Bishop of Hermopolis.

Marquise Lenore turned pale.

"She had one of her migraines yesterday!" exclaimed the Princess. "Ask Gaston about that, when he comes, Your Lordship."

"Is the story so very terrible?" asked the Archbishop.

"Yes, it is very terrible... let it be... you'll make me ill!"

It was like throwing a cup of water on a raging fire. A hundred voices were raised–among which, to tell the truth, those of the two prelates were included.

"There's a story here!"

"Oh, Madame la Marquise, please! Do tell!"

Lenore smiled sadly. "Mother," she said to the Princess, "I can't refuse these women the finale of a drama in which they have played a role–but the denouement is horrible; I ask your permission to cut the story short."

"Not too short!" they implored. The word horrible is not nearly as intimidating as it is believed to be.

The charming Marquise de Lorgères collected herself for a moment, then began: "Did the person who took the name of Baron von Altenheimer, in relating the incident that caused the ruination of my father, happen to mention a young girl named Efflam, who was my friend and companion?"

"Yes indeed," came the reply from all sides. "Efflam, the young Magyar girl, whose parents lived at the Turkish border: one of the vampire's victims!"

"A poor angel who has her rightful place in Heaven," Lenore replied, in a melancholy tone. "Efflam's father left Petrovaradin after his daughter's death; his wife did not survive her grief. He went to live in an isolated cabin in the middle of the Great Hungarian Plain. He was in great distress.

"He had heard tell of the two black graves that were sometimes occupied by the bodies of the Chevalier Ténèbre and his brother Ange, the vampire, who were forced to return at least once a year to their mortuary domicile. He had heard, too, that if it were possible to take them by surprise and burn their hearts with a red-hot iron, the world would be freed forever from those two monsters.

"He waited for his opportunity. He went out every morning to lift up the black marble slabs which covered the two graves..."

"So these two graves actually exist?" Archbishop de Quélen asked.

"Certainly," the Princess replied. "I saw them myself while I was there for the wedding... one great and one small, with the inscriptions you know."

"One day last April," Lenore went on, "during a hunting-party in the Chandor forest, two assassination attempts were made against the person of the Marquis de Lorgères, and that same evening my father was told that the brothers Ténèbre were in the vicinity. It is necessary to tell you, at the risk of diminishing the interest of the story somewhat, that the Chevalier Ténèbre is an old employee of the London police, and that his brother Ange, the vampire, came straight from Botany Bay, whence he had been transported as a common thief. The chevalier was named William Moore and the vampire Bob or Bobby Bobson. A few weeks after the adventure I want to relate to you, Szeged was full of police officers from London, following the trail of our two phantoms.

"My father put the whole household on horseback, arming the entire force, in order to search the area. The chase began as night was falling. At two o'clock in the morning, the fugitives were recognized, but they slipped out of sight until morning, when their tracks were found and followed. The trail led my father and his troop into the middle of the Great Hungarian Plain, more than twenty leagues from Chandor. There, it ended. One might have thought that the two fugitives had vanished into thin air. My father and his men returned to the castle on the following day, after a day of futile searching.

"That night, however, when our men had gone, David Kuntz, the father of my poor Efflam, went, as was his custom, to lift the marble tombstones.

"Under the first, he saw a sleeping man; under the second, another in the same state. He sharpened a plowshare in order that he might heat it up and plunge it, as was their due, into the hearts of the oupire and the vampire, but his courage failed him. Instead, he went to find huge and heavy rocks, which he deposited on the slabs of black marble in such a fashion that no human force would be able to disturb them again. Afterwards, he spent several days collecting bits of wood, dry vegetation and straw, an enormous quantity of which he piled up above and around the two graves.

"Each time that he returned, he heard voices coming from the ground, asking him for mercy, but he paid them no heed.

"The voices gradually became fainter. The one which came from the larger grave fell silent first, then the other faded in its turn. They had pleaded for twenty-eight hours each.

"The pile of combustible material was now as high as a two-story house. David Kuntz set it alight. It burned, and continued smoldering for three days. It took a further three days for the tombstones and the surrounding earth to cool down again. It was, in consequence, not until the seventh day after the fire that David Kuntz was able to take the rocks away and lift the marble tombstones. He found beneath them two human corpses–one tall and one short–which had kept their shape, but were now the color of charcoal. When he put out his hands to touch them, the two corpses fell into dust..."

"And since that moment," added the Princess, "you will understand that nothing more has been heard of the brothers Ténèbre."

As she finished, the prefect of police came in, followed by Gaston and his father-in-law, Prince Jacobyi. The Prince seemed anxious; Gaston's face had a mortal pallor.

"My Ladies," asked the prefect of police, "do you remember those two audacious bandits who robbed our *protégés* in the Holy Land, at this very same event last year?"

The question sounded so strange, after the tale told by Lenore, that it was met by a profound silence.

"Their exploits are following the same course," the prefect continued, in a light tone. "Here is a newspaper from The Hague, which tells of their latest tour de force. Anna Paulowna, the Princess Royal and Princess of Orange, was robbed of her diamonds in broad daylight, and in their place in the jewel-case was a visiting card: an old Flemish woodcut depicting two men, one tall and one short, the tall one wearing armor and the short one costumed as a priest. Under the former were the words Le Chevalier Ténèbre; under the latter Brother Ange, the Vampire..."

There was a protracted murmur in the hall, which covered the voice of Prince Jacobyi asking of his son-in-law: "Will you let me see that letter?"

Gaston, without replying, unfolded a piece of paper that he had crumpled in his hand. The Prince took it and read:

See you soon!

And by way of signature:

The tall one and the short one.

A Brief Afterword

The chimerical combination of attributes possessed by *Knightshade* can be seen in various other works produced according to the "Galland formula" that Paul Féval was likely to have read. Two of its most important predecessors had been written in French by foreign noblemen. The earlier of these two, *Les Quatre Facardins* (tr. as *The Four Facardins*), which Count Antony Hamilton left unfinished at his death in 1720, is an affectionate parody written shortly after the appearance of Galland's translation, whose cheerful humor must have appealed to Féval as the work of a kindred spirit. The later had only been published in fragmentary form, and its attribution to the Polish count Jan Potocki–though correct–seemed far from certain at the time, but its importance was already established and its influence on *Knightshade* is very marked. The work is properly titled *Le Manuscrit Trouvé à Saragossa* (*The Manuscript Found at Saragossa*), although it is more often referred to as *The Saragossa Manuscript*. The two portions that had been published in Paris in Féval's day were (in their correct narrative order) *Dix Journées de la Vie d'Alphonse van Worden* (1814) and *Avadoro, Histoire Espagnole* (1813).

Potocki's crucial contribution to the Galland formula was a calculated blurring of the boundary between the real and the imaginary; his hero, Alphonse van Worden, goes to sleep near a gibbet where two infamous brigands have been hanged, and is thereafter uncertain which of his awakenings are real and which merely illusory. It appears that the two hanged men are continually appearing and disappearing, perhaps transforming themselves into two beautiful women who might or might not be vampiric *succubi*. As time goes by, though, the highly fanciful and horrific opening sequence gives way to a series of mundane accounts of the criminal and romantic exploits of the bandit Avadoro and other key members of his extended family.

Although Féval did not appropriate Potocki's chief innovation, he does seem to have taken many of the other elements of his own tale from Potocki. The tale told by Baron von Altenheimer similarly features two exceedingly restless hanged men, one of them allegedly a vampire, and it too is transformed by degrees into an account of prodigious but mundane banditry. Whereas Alphonse van Worden is continually harassed by the question of what is real, however, the Baron's listeners–and, more particularly, the audience of readers eavesdropping on his hearers–is tickled and tormented by the less grandiose question of what is true.

Potocki's hero is confused by his uncertainty as to what he has really experienced and what he has only dreamed, and so are his readers. The reader within the text, like those without, is confronted with a written page which can only be taken at face value. Féval's Princess de Montfort and Marquis de Lorgères are, by contrast, listening to a story told by another character, the Baron von Altenheimer. When the Baron's brother reveals that the two brothers who featured as tellers of the tale within the Baron's tale were the protagonists of their own tale, the brothers Ténèbre, in disguise, the clear implication—even though the hearers of the tale do not pick it up–is that the Baron and his brother are the very same protagonists. This addition of a new layer of deception is, however, open to two rival interpretations.

The fact that the Baron and his brother are the tellers of the tale of the gypsy brothers, who were themselves the leading characters of their own tale, the brothers Ténèbre, might mean that the Baron and his brother are also the brothers Ténèbre–but it might also mean that they are common-or-garden scoundrels who are merely employing the fanciful tale of the brothers Ténèbre as a literary device to entrance and confound listeners whom they intend to rob.

Although no one in Paris knew it in 1860, Jan Potocki did eventually provide his Gallandesque story with a resolution, albeit an unconvincing one. Many readers, however, still prefer the partial version, which suggests by its incompleteness that no resolution is even conceivable. Perhaps Féval took that view, although his own approach to the conservation of ambiguity is to scatter possible keys to the interpretation of his narrative hither and yon with merry abandon. One, in particular, deserves special consideration.

Perhaps, the Baron suggests at one point, we should not view the brothers Ténèbre as unusually resilient criminals, but rather as incarnations of two of the seven deadly sins, which are bound to rear their ugly heads again and again no matter how securely conscience might seek to bury them. This seems to be the best interpretation of what "actually happens" in the final phases of the plot, when the pattern of bathetic reduction is suddenly thrown into reverse.

If we try to make sense of the story by asking whether the brothers Ténèbre were "really" supernaturally powered brigands, one of whom had a blood-drinking habit, or whether they were "really" English con-men with fabulous storytelling skills, we shall not only fail to make sense of it but will miss the point entirely. They are more akin to the moral equivalent of elemental spirits, one (Avarice) tall and powerful, the other (Lust), effeminate and seductive. The can be defeated in the short term, but no matter what palliative rituals are followed in the wake of their temporary burial, they will always be back. Their earthly representatives may be increasingly vulgar, but they are no less irrepressible for that; as the Baron points out when first entrancing his audience, the great brigands of yore may have been replaced by vulgar thieves, but the latter make up in sheer quantity what they lack in individual quality. Indeed, it may be a mistake to aggrandize Avarice and Lust as monstrous demonic powers, because such characterization may deflect attention away from their ever presence in our midst.

Knightshade did not give rise to a series; nor is it a long story by comparison with Galland's *Arabian Nights* or Potocki's *Saragossa Manuscript*, but there is a sense in which it is part of a series, and nests within the greatest compendium of stories there is, because it recognizes and observes that villainy always wears the same faces–that whoever listens to stories like those within the story always finds the brothers Ténèbre familiar, and cannot find its ultimate conclusion surprising.

The brothers Ténèbre come back at the end because the brothers Ténèbre always come back, if not in one guise then another; their visits are always expensive; and they are always recognizable, if only we could use our eyes efficiently. They are the Eternal Adversaries against which Eternal Champions and Thousand-Faced Heroes are pitched–and whose existence not only necessitates but justifies the existence of those who stand against them.

They do not "make sense"–but that is their very essence, and the ultimate secret of their identity.

Notes

[1] Like the other ancestral lists with which the novella is peppered, this one serves to emphasize the continuity between the aristocratic society of the early 19th century and the persons and events which had shaped European history during the preceding centuries. Féval, a Breton himself, had a particular fondness for the great families of that region. The list ends with the names of the last king of Brittany, François II (1435-1488) and his daughter Anne, who enjoyed a brief rule before the duchy was more fully absorbed into the rapidly-evolving French nation.

[2] François de Harlay de Champvallon (1625-1695) became Archbishop of Paris in 1671. Charles Maurice de Talleyrand-Périgord (1754-1838) was one of the foremost and most versatile Frenchmen of his era: a Churchman, a statesmen and a diplomat. He was a leading figure in the Revolution before helping Napoleon take power, but subsequently fell out with the Emperor and took a prominent part in the Bourbon Restoration before also taking a hand in the Revolution of 1830.

[3] Wurtemburg became a major European state in 1495, when the duchy was established, but it only became a kingdom after its conquest by Napoleon and it was gradually absorbed into the evolving German nation during the 19th century, exemplifying one aspect of the pattern of historical change to which Féval is calling attention.

[4] Rob Roy was a famous Scottish outlaw of the early 18th century, immortalized by Sir Walter Scott's eponymous novel. Schinderhannes was the alias of the German brigand Johann Bückler, who was hanged at Mainz in 1803. Louis Mandrin was an 18th-century French brigand whose campaign against tax-collectors made him a folk hero; his name was often coupled with that of Louis Dominique Cartouche, the leader of another famous robber band; both were eventually captured and broken on the wheel. According to Charles Mackay's essay on "Popular Admiration of Great Thieves" in *Extraordinary Popular Delusions and the Madness of Crowds* (1852)–which Féval might have read and from which he might have taken some inspiration, Schubry was a Hungarian brigand, but Zawn is not mentioned there and I can find no other reference to him.

[5] Fra Diavolo was the nickname of Michele Pezza, or Pozzo, an Italian robber turned Bourbon partisan, who was hanged in Naples in 1806 by General Hugo. Paul Féval gave the character a starring role in *Les Habits Noirs*.

[6] This translation is taken from the Marabout paperback edition of 1972, which reprinted the text of the 1875 book. I do not know whether, or to what extent, that version varies from the original serial version of 1860, but it might be worth noting that the Franco-Prussian war of 1870 (in which Wurtemburg sided with Prussia) occurred in the interim. It would not be surprising if Féval had taken the opportunity to import a little extra anti-German sentiment into the book version, but neither

would it have been unusual to find this kind of stereo-
typing in a French popular magazine in 1860.

[7] Paillasse is the French version of the Italian Pagliacci:
the epitome of the sad clown.

[8] The German writer Ernst Theodor Amadeus Hoffmann (1776-1822) was the most significant pioneer of
modern horror fiction, usually keeping a fine balance
between psychological and supernatural interpretations
of the grotesqueries featured in his tales.

[9] Matthias I, Corvinus, a.k.a. "The Great" (1443-1490),
the younger son of John Hunyadi (see note 12), was king
of Hungary from 1458-90. He was perennially engaged
in wars against the Turks, the Bohemians, the Poles and
the Holy Roman Emperor.

[10] Hospodar was a title originally borne by the princes
or governors of Walachia and Moldavia when they were
vassals of the Turkish Sultan; it was retained long afterwards by Lithuanian princes and Polish kings.

[11] The city of Semlin-Zimony in Hungarian–Zemun in
Serbian–was situated on the bank of the Danube opposite to Belgrade; it was eventually swallowed up by its
larger neighbor. The town which Féval calls Itèbe presumably suffered a similar fate as I have been unable to
locate a likely candidate on modern maps. In general I
have followed the policy of substituting the current
names of the Hungarian and Rumanian geographical
features for those that Féval uses–e.g. Tisza for his The-

171

iss, Petrovaradin for his Peterwardein, Timisoara for his Temesvar–but where this proved impractical I have let his versions stand. I have used "the Great Hungarian Plain" (which is clearer than "the Great Alföld" or "Nagy Magyar Alföld") where Féval refers to the plain of "Grand-Waraden," since the province of Warasdin is long gone.

[12] John Hunyadi (1407-1456) was the scion of a noble Hungarian family, who became voivode of Transylvania and Captain of Belgrade, in which capacity he waged war against the Turks. He won a famous victory over Mezid Bey in the last year of his life–the year in which Vlad the Impaler first became ruler of Walachia.

[13] Although the modern name of this city is Smederevo, the old name still survives so I have let it stand.

[14] As with the other ancestral lists, the family names employed here are real, but the particular individuals are not. The Barberinis were a notable Roman family who had become extinct in 1738. Féval used the Policenis in *Les Habits Noirs*.

[15] Charles Edward Stuart the "Young Pretender," also known as Bonnie Prince Charlie, had settled in Italy in 1766 and died there–childless, so far as anyone knows– in 1788. Charles's younger brother Henry, who supported him during the Jacobite rebellion, styled himself Henry IX thereafter, until his own death in 1807. Henry was unlikely to have been involved in plotting against against Charles–although a man of Henry's conspicuous piety could hardly help disapproving of his brother's dissolute lifestyle–but if Charles had had a son,

Henry's claim to be the rightful King of England from 1788-1809 would have been falser than it actually was.

[16] King Wilhelm I was one of the longest-reigning monarchs of 19th-century Europe, occupying the throne from 1816-1864.

[17] The French invaded Spain in 1823 and fought a crucial battle at the Trocadero which won them entry to Cadiz.

[18] Prince Klemens von Metternich (1773-1859) was one of the leading statesmen of the early 19th century. He eventually became a leading opponent of Napoleon, having studied the Emperor carefully while he was Austrian minister to France in 1806-8. Metternich was the main architect of the Austrian Empire re-constructed after Napoleon's defeat, but his influence began to wane after 1825. There is considerable symbolic significance in this mutual recognition by key representatives of the old and new aristocracies of Europe that the symbols of their wealth and power have been stolen.

[19] Jean-François Lesueur (1760-1837) was the outstanding French composer of religious music during the early 19th century and a famous teacher–Berlioz and Gounod were among his pupils.

[20] Jean-Baptiste Isabey (1767-1855) was a celebrated miniaturist, Madame de Mirbel was presumably the wife of Charles François Brisseau de Mirbel (1776-1854), a

botanist. Jean Petitot (1607-1691) was a Swiss painter noted for his work in enamel.

[21] Condé was the family name of the Ducs de Bourbon.

[22] The name *zouave* was borrowed from an Algerian tribe for application to members of French infantry regiments whose brightly-colored uniforms included baggy trousers, short jackets and tasseled caps. Although the regiments in question were originally made up of Algerians, they soon had a majority of Frenchmen. When he wrote the story Féval, would not have known that the uniform would be borrowed by some volunteer regiments on the Union side in the American Civil War, but he would have appreciated the absurdity.

[23] The apparatus in question, invented in 1836, was the work of the English chemist James Marsh (1794-1846).

[24] In view of the highly unlikely first name, it seems probable that this gentleman is an invention of Féval's, although it is not beyond the bounds of possibility that some such character might have been featured in the Newgate Calendar or the "broadside ballads" that chronicled the adventures of British criminals in the late 18th and early 19th centuries. It was, of course, the Newgate Calendar and its literary spin-off that made Jack Sheppard the most famous English thief of his era. Féval might have read William Harrison Ainsworth's *Jack Sheppard* (Bentley, 1839), a novel similar in spirit to Suesque *romans feuilletons*.

[25] Charles Kemble (1775-1854) was the leading British actor of the period; François-Joseph Talma (1763-1826) was his French counterpart.

[26] The Roman Catholic Church celebrates St. Sylvester's Day, as might be deduced from the context, on the thirty-first of December. There is, however, a neat irony concealed in this mode of expression, because the Eastern Churches celebrate St. Sylvester's Day on the second of January.

[27] Baron Guillaume Dupuytren (1777-1835) was the leading French surgeon and anatomist of his day. Although surgery was a nasty business in the days before effective anesthetics, when cauterization was the only effective ward against infection, surgeons usually did more good than physicians, most of whose remedies were impotent or dangerous. Féval's sarcastic treatment of Doctor Récamier's favored panacea of "cold affusions taken in warm baths"–i.e., pouring cold water over a patient sitting in a warm bath–is reasonably good-humored because he knew well enough that the "treatments" favored by most quacks were likely to make matters worse.

[28] The French district which includes Chartres.

[29] Eighty kilometers, or fifty miles.

[30] "Jean Raisin" can be translated as "John Grape"–an imaginary character of a lower social class, as well as a more urban disposition, than the Classical god of the

Bacchanal. The Seine town of Bercy, as the first chapter of the story also pointed out, was the site of the warehouses where wood and wine bound for Paris was stored. Suresnes was the neighboring wine-producing region, formerly famed for its quality but notorious by the time at which Féval was writing for vintages so poor that the first (1872) edition of Larousse described them as *"très-laxatif et très-médiocre."* The reference to Courtille has to be seen in the context of the previous sarcastic reference to a 360-day Carnival. (Properly speaking, of course, Carnival–derived from the Latin "farewell to meat"–refers to the last few days before the beginning of the Lenten fast, especially to the final *Mardi Gras*, or "fat Tuesday," when the last remaining meat-products had to be consumed.) One of the more remarkable and less salubrious manifestations of the Paris Carnival in the mid-19th century was the so-called *"descente de la Courtille,"* a procession through that district of Paris, which was then notorious for its cabarets and dance halls.

Also by Paul Féval
translated, annotated and introduced by
Brian Stableford

VAMPIRE CITY

Some tell of a great city of black jasper which has streets
and buildings like any other city but is eternally in
mourning, enveloped by perpetual gloom... Some call it
Selene, some Vampire City, but the vampires refer to it
among themselves by the name of the Sepulchre... To
destroy the dreaded vampire lord Otto Goetzi, writer
Ann Radcliffe, Merry Bones the Irishman, and Grey
Jack, her faithful servant, launch an all-out attack on
Selene...

"*We can easily see in* Vampire City *the ultimate literary
ancestor of* Buffy the Vampire-Slayer," writes Stableford.

200 pages – ISBN 0-9740711-6-1 – $19.95

THE VAMPIRE COUNTESS

In vita mors, in morte vita! In life, death; in death, life! The particular gift of Countess Addhema was to be re-born beautiful and young every time she could apply to the hideous bareness of her skull a living head of hair, a scalp, torn from the head of a living victim. This was why her tomb was full of the skulls of young women... René recoiled in horror at the sight of his mistress restored to her real condition: the cadaver of an old woman, fleshless, cold, totally bald and already turning to dust...

"*After 1856, it would be a long time before any other writer contrived a vampire as perversely charismatic as Addhema; she is really three vampires in one. She is, first and foremost, the vampire-as-libido-run-wild, but she is certainly the vampire-as-gold-digger too, and she may well have something of the vampire-as-muse to complete her mystique,*" writes Stableford.

352 pages – ISBN 0-9740711-4-5 – $22.95

Brian Stableford has been a professional writer since 1965. He has published more than 50 novels and two hundred short stories, as well as several non-fiction books, thousands of articles for periodicals and reference books, several volumes of translations from the French and a number of anthologies. He is also a part-time Lecturer in Creative Writing at King Alfred's College Winchester. His novels include *The Empire of Fear* (1988), *Young Blood* (1992) and his future history series comprising *Inherit the Earth* (1998), *Architects of Emortality* (1999), *The Fountains of Youth* (2000), *The Cassandra Complex* (2001), *Dark Ararat* (2002) and *The Omega Expedition* (2002). His non-fiction includes *Scientific Romance in Britain* (1985), *Teach Yourself Writing Fantasy and Science Fiction* (1997), *Yesterday's Bestsellers* (1998) and *Glorious Perversity: The Decline and Fall of Literary Decadence* (1998). His anthologies include *The Dedalus Book of Decadence (Moral Ruins)* (1990) and *The Dedalus Book of British Fantasy* (1991). Reference books to which he has contributed include the Clute/Nicholls *Encyclopedia of Science Fiction* (1979; 2nd ed. 1993), Neil Barron's *Anatomy of Wonder* (2nd. ed. 1981; 3rd ed. 1987; 4th ed. 1995) and *The Cambridge Guide to Literature in English* (1988; 2nd ed 1993). Due in the near future are *Kiss the Goat: A Twenty-first Century Ghost Story* (Prime Press) and a collection of translations of stories by Villiers de l'Isle Adam, *Claire Lenoir and Other Stories* (Tartarus Press). His current projects include the compilation a *Historical Dictionary of Science Fiction Literature* for Scarecrow Press.

www.ingramcontent.com/pod-product-compliance
Lightning Source LLC
Chambersburg PA
CBHW030506260626
47157CB00005B/1680